Also by Bella Forrest:

A SHADE OF VAMPIRE SERIES:

A Shade of Vampire (Book 1)

A Shade of Blood (Book 2)

A Castle of Sand (Book 3)

A Shadow of Light (Book 4)

A Blaze of Sun (Book 5)

A Gate of Night (Book 6)

A Break of Day (Book 7)

A Shade of Novak (Book 8)

A SHADE OF KIEV TRILOGY:

A Shade of Kiev 1

A Shade of Kiev 2

A Shade of Kiev 3

BEAUTIFUL MONSTER DUOLOGY:

Beautiful Monster 1

Beautiful Monster 2

For an updated list of Bella's books,
please visit www.bellaforrest.net

Contents

Chapter 1: Mona

Kiev's lips touched the back of my neck as I lay against him, his steady breathing chilling my skin.

We didn't exchange a word for hours. Now that the heat of the moment had passed, the weight of what we had just done was beginning to settle upon me.

I wondered what he was thinking.

I swallowed back the lump in my throat and ran my fingers along his arm, which rested around my waist.

"Thank you, Kiev," I whispered.

He exhaled and withdrew his arm. I turned around to see him roll onto his back and fix his eyes on the ceiling.

"What?" I leant my chin on his bare shoulder, gazing up at him.

"I'm not sure that you should be thanking me."

I sat up and leaned my back against the wall, drawing my knees up against my chest. I felt suddenly too bare before him and covered myself with a sheet.

I understood his response. I was fully aware of the gravity of our situation. And yet I couldn't help but feel thankful to him for this glass of water in the desert. Even if it only made me thirstier.

He stood up and wrapped a towel around his waist. He headed out to the balcony, placing both hands on the banister. Bunching the sheet around me, I followed him.

I placed a hand over his cold one. Finally, he looked me in the eye.

"I feel thankful all the same."

"Even though I didn't do any of this for you?"

I took a step backward, trying to read his serious expression.

"What do you mean?"

He turned his back on me and reached up to the top of the doorframe. His muscular back arched as he leaned against it.

"I did this for myself," he said. "I didn't give a second's thought to how this might impact you. So don't thank me."

The words he had spoken before we'd made love echoed around in my head.

"I'm not here to comfort you... All I know is that I needed to

see you again."

I crossed my arms over my chest, feeling goosebumps on my skin as a chilly breeze blew across the lake.

"What are you trying to say?"

He whirled around, his green eyes settling on me.

"Could I make myself any clearer?" he snapped. "I'm not looking out for your best interests. So don't thank me. It's absurd."

I was trying to wrap my head around what he was saying. Why he was saying it.

"So you'd prefer me to be angry and call you a selfish bastard."

His tone was beginning to grate on my nerves.

"That would be more appropriate and certainly less delusional."

We both stood still, glaring at each other.

Then something sparked in his eyes. His breath hitched. He closed the distance between us, wrapping one arm around my waist while the other hand reached into my hair. As he pulled my head back, his lips began kneading harshly against mine.

My own passions took over despite myself. I let go of the sheet covering me and wrapped both arms around his neck, pulling myself up against him and locking my legs around him as I responded to his kiss.

We were both breathing heavily again as our lips broke

apart minutes later.

"What are we?" I whispered.

He lowered me back down to the ground.

"I don't know."

I stared at him for several moments longer, but unsure what to say, I walked back into the cabin. I found a dress in my old cupboard and slipped it over my head. Kiev picked up his own torn clothes from the floor and put them on.

I walked up to him and placed my hand in his, tugging at him to follow me outside again.

He didn't ask where I was leading him as I walked to the edge of the balcony. Gripping his hand more tightly, I vanished us both back to the mainland.

We still had time before we had to return to The Shade, and I just wanted to walk with him. That little cabin had suddenly felt too small and claustrophobic for the two of us.

I didn't know where I was going to take him. But walking, rather than standing still, felt like what I needed to be doing. It distracted me from the pain that was beginning to eat away at me as each second of our short time together ebbed away.

As we neared the entrance of what used to be the vampires' tunnels, before Kiev's siblings made Matteo and his crew evacuate, Kiev darted off into the forest.

What in the world…

Someone screamed.

My mouth dropped open and all the blood drained from my face as Kiev emerged from the woods, gripping a young woman by the neck.

"Celice!" I gasped.

My stomach jumped to my throat as I stared at her sweaty face.

As Kiev dragged her closer, he grunted and let go of her as if he'd just been burned.

Celice stood up straight, a look of triumph on her face.

Kiev launched at her again, but she raised her hands and put up a forcefield around her. He couldn't come within a few feet of her.

"You," she said gleefully to me, "are in some serious trouble for stealing this vampire from me. He was supposed to be mine. Not yours. You already have Rhys. He's not going to be too pleased when I return and tell him all about—"

The curse escaped my lips before I could stop it. A bolt of fire shot from my palms, breaking through the young witch's forcefield and hitting her square in the chest. She crashed back against a tree. Sliding down its trunk, her body was limp as she hit the ground.

My limbs trembled as I stared in disbelief.

What have I done?

I staggered toward her, gripping her head in my hands. Her eyes were open, staring blankly ahead. I laid her down on the forest ground and placed my ear against her chest.

Not even the slightest hint of a heartbeat.

Kiev approached beside me. He looked almost as shocked as I felt.

And then he voiced what I was hoping wasn't true.

"She's dead."

Chapter 2: Kiev

I stared at the corpse. It had all happened so fast. The snapping of twigs, the dark brown curls above a bush, a sharp intake of breath…

I should have suspected Celice when I heard that sound on the balcony back in the castle.

"I killed her." Mona's breathing came in short rasps as she got to her feet and stumbled away from the body. "I d-don't know what I was thinking."

I bent down and scooped up Celice's body in my arms.

"What are you doing?" Mona gripped my arm.

I brushed her away.

"We shouldn't leave her body here in the open."

I began walking back down to the lake. Mona followed

me, still in shock.

Once I reached the bank, I placed the body down on the ground. Removing my shirt, I ripped off a strip of fabric. I picked up a stone and tied one end of the cotton around it, fastening the other to Celice's ankle.

"Y-you're going to dump her in the lake?" Mona looked at me in horror.

"Why not? The fish will eat away her flesh soon enough."

Picking up both Celice and the rock, I waded into the water. I swam with both until I reached the center where I let go, watching as the brunette's body disappeared into the lake's depths.

I returned to the bank.

"Dry me," I said to Mona, who was still staring at the center of the lake where I had dropped the body. I shook her shoulders. "I said dry me."

She came to her senses and dried me, although her voice trembled even as she uttered the charm.

"W-we need to leave here," she said. She threw one last look at the lake, and then her deep blue eyes settled on me. Before I could respond, she grasped my hands and in a whirl of colors we had disappeared from Matteo's island.

A few seconds later, I opened my eyes to find us both standing back on The Shade's beach, close to the port.

I looked down at Mona.

"I need to get back to the castle," was all she said.

Taking a step away from me, she vanished.

I stood still, my eyes fixed on the sand where now only her footprints remained. I decided to wait before returning so that we arrived back at different times.

I breathed in the sea air, turning to face the waves.

Mona... I don't know what I'm doing any more. This was probably a mistake. Soon enough, Mona will be another woman whose downfall I'll be responsible for.

Yet I still wanted to see her.

I thought of Rhys and wondered how much longer it would be before he returned with more humans. I guessed that he probably wouldn't be back for at least another half day.

We'd returned early, Mona and I. Thanks to that little wench.

I still felt surprised by the force of Mona's spell. I'd been so used to thinking of Mona as helpless—no different really than a human. Seeing her display such prowess was strange. But something about it brought me comfort—it made her seem less fragile, less breakable. Unlike all the previous women in my life.

As I continued walking along the beach, I wondered if Celice could have already told Rhys and her sisters about us. Somehow, I doubted it. If Rhys knew, Mona would have known about it. On that front at least, we were safe.

Then there was the issue of the human disappearances.

The only way Rhys would suspect me was if Tiarni mentioned we'd both been on the island together. But I doubted that would happen—since I'd gotten Tiarni so drunk that night, she couldn't be sure that she hadn't left the cell doors open by accident.

Even if Tiarni was lucid enough to realize that I had done it—especially since it had happened both in The Shade and their island in quick succession—it would still be my word against hers because she had no evidence. That could of course lead both of us into an awkward situation with Rhys. He didn't strike me as the most charitable of sorts.

I'll just have to deal with it when it happens. What's done is done.

All this trouble for that witch. And why? I still didn't even understand myself.

I still didn't understand what drew me to her. Why I wanted her so. Why I was willing to risk so much just to see her.

After half an hour, I left the beach and walked back though the woods to the castle.

I headed straight to my quarters. Thankfully nobody saw me on my way up, for I was wearing no shirt and my pants were torn.

I locked the door and went into the bathroom to take a shower, careful to inspect my body and clothes for Mona's long blonde hairs. I threw away my old clothes and put on fresh ones. Then I lay down on the bed and stared up at the ceiling.

I had touched another corpse today.

Only this time, I had not claimed the life myself.

I wondered if this day was the first time Mona had killed. Although she'd appeared to feel guilty afterward, she certainly hadn't seemed to have any qualms while she was doing it.

Killing seemed second nature to her.

Chapter 3: Mona

As soon as I arrived back in Rhys' apartment, I rushed to take a shower. I soaped myself from top to bottom and washed my hair to rid myself of Kiev's scent. I changed into a clean dress and vanished my old clothes.

I was still in a state of shock as I paced up and down the apartment, trying to wrap my mind around what had just transpired.

I couldn't believe that Celice was dead. But most of all, I couldn't understand how I could have killed her. Rhys had taught me fatal curses in the past, but that was a long time ago. What disturbed me was how instinctively that curse had come to my lips. I'd thought that I'd forgotten how to even perform such powerful magic, yet it had come to me without even having to think.

I just murdered Rhys' sister. His youngest sister. Rhys always had been most affectionate with and protective of his youngest sister.

Still shaking, I got into bed and pulled the covers over me. I closed my eyes, trying to steady my mind. Trying to numb the guilt that was tearing at my chest.

The door clicked open at some point past midnight.

Rhys entered. He whipped off his cloak and swung it over a chair. His dark eyes roamed me as I lay in bed.

"H-how did it go?" I asked, trying to keep my voice from breaking.

"A disaster." He scowled.

I sat up, trying to assume a look of concern.

"Why were you gone so long? What happened?"

He sat down on the bed and removed his heavy boots. Leaning back against the headboard, he stretched out his legs on the mattress.

"The humans were gone from our island too. The dungeon's door had been left open. Some of the old boats were gone."

I clasped a hand to my mouth and gasped.

"But how?"

"We don't know. But it's clear now that we have a rat among us."

He stripped to his underwear and slipped between the

covers, lying next to me. He didn't stop eyeing me as he rested his head on the pillow. He reached out and gripped the back of my head, pulling me closer against him.

"You wouldn't happen to know anything about this?" His voice was soft but deadly.

My heart beat faster.

"How would I?"

Silence.

I sat up and stared down at him, doing my best to act indignant.

"How could you think I could have done this?"

"You've been acting strangely ever since we arrived on this island."

I shook my head.

"I had nothing to do with this. I promise you."

He continued staring at me.

Finally, he reached for me and pulled me against him.

Desperate to change the subject, I asked, "So you had to get a new batch of humans?"

"Hm."

Although I was still curious, I didn't dare ask where he got them from. It didn't matter at that point.

"I need to rest now," he said, rolling over onto his side. "It's been a long day. And tomorrow may be even longer. I'm going to smoke out this rat."

He reached out to the bedside table and switched off the

light.

I lay trapped in his arms as I listened to him drift off.

Smoke out the rat.

What's he going to do?

I realized how flimsy Kiev's cover was. If anyone found out that he had gone with Tiarni to the island—and I was sure Rhys would sooner or later—Tiarni could reveal what happened. And even if she didn't, Kiev would be under suspicion. That was something I couldn't allow, especially now that Celice had also mysteriously disappeared.

"Oh, by the way," Rhys said. "Have you seen Celice recently? Julisse and Arielle said they've been looking everywhere for her."

"No," I said. "I can't imagine where she's got to."

Chapter 4: Kiev

I was woken by a knock on my front door.

Groaning, I staggered out of bed. I wrapped a robe around me and opened the door.

My brother stood in the doorway, his arms crossed over his chest.

"Erik?"

His mouth hung open as soon as he saw me.

"Your eyes! They… they're green."

I heaved a sigh.

"Yes."

"How?"

"I don't know. They change every now and then. What was it you wanted?"

Still staring at my eyes, he said, "You're going to be late for lunch. It's in five minutes."

"I'm not hungry."

I motioned to close the door, but he held out his hand. "Rhys' orders."

I scowled.

"All right. I'll be down."

I closed the door and pulled on some clothes before heading down to the dining room. The high-ceilinged hall was already almost full with vampires and witches. I made my way over to the end of the table where I took a seat in between Helina and Erik.

"Kiev! Your eyes," Helina gasped as soon as she saw me. "They're green!"

"Yes, I'm aware," I said dryly, rubbing my temples.

"How?"

I gave her the same answer I'd given Erik. And before she could ask more questions, Rhys stood up and raised his hands for silence.

I glanced briefly at Mona. She sat next to Rhys, her eyes fixed on her plate. Her face was ashen.

Silence fell upon the hall.

"I assume the word has got out already." His eyes traveled along the table. "We have a traitor in our midst."

I stared right back at him as his gaze reached me. He didn't linger on me any longer than the others.

"What I thought might have been a foolish mistake is now clearly much more. Somebody released the humans on our island just after the humans here went missing. Since the Novalics have been unsuccessful at finding the culprit, Efren and I will take over from here. We will be interrogating each and every one of you. We will get to the bottom of this, so I suggest that you admit it now rather than drawing out the pain. Because we will find you."

Mona's hand clenched around her fork. Helina tensed beside me.

I kept my breathing calm and steady as I watched Rhys.

"Interrogations will be conducted in here. We'll begin directly after lunch." He turned to the right of the table and pointed to the first two vampires sitting there. "You two will be first." He looked back at everyone else. "Make sure you've finished eating by two o'clock sharp. Nightly rituals will also be paused until we've caught this traitor."

Rhys sat back down and continued to glare at us.

I swallowed back three glasses of blood and stood up. I didn't give Helina the chance to hold me back. I melded in with a group of vampires hurrying out of the hall. I slipped out of the entrance and walked around the back of the castle, where one was less likely to bump into people.

I needed some fresh air to clear my head.

If I was to be suspected, it would be due to Tiarni. I needed to make sure she wouldn't tell. Because if she did, although I wasn't particularly worried about what would happen to me, it would affect my siblings.

A hiss came from behind me.

"Kiev!"

Mona stood ten feet away from me. She wore black gloves and a cloak over her long dress. I closed the distance between us.

Her eyes were wide. "I need to meet you back in your room. While Rhys is busy with the interrogation. Go there now. I'll follow in five minutes."

She turned and walked away.

I did as she requested and returned to my apartment.

She knocked on the door a few minutes later.

"Tiarni," she breathed.

I nodded.

"Have her here in your room by ten o'clock tonight. I don't have time to explain. Just do it."

She turned to leave. I reached out to grab her hand.

"Leave me."

"What are you planning?"

She struggled against me. "I don't have time to—"

"You'll kill her too?"

She stopped struggling and stared at me for several moments.

Her lips parted, and I thought she was about to answer. But then she vanished into thin air.

Chapter 5: Mona

Rhys didn't pay attention to me for most of the day. He was busy interrogating vampires and witches, and then scouring the island along with his two sisters in search of Celice.

I spent most of my day round the back of the castle, watching the entrance to the island's underground spell room. Efren was in there for hours and I was beginning to lose hope that he'd ever leave, but finally he emerged from the trapdoor, leaving me less than two hours to concoct the potion I needed for later that night.

I ducked down further into the bushes, waiting with bated breath until he'd disappeared from sight. Then I crept toward the door. I fumbled around for the clasp and lifted it up. I hurried down the steps and shut the door over me. I had to hope that none of the witches would need to use the room for the next couple of hours. If someone came in and asked what I was concocting, I'd just have to make something up.

I looked around the dim circular chamber. A rusty smell of human blood wafted into my nostrils. Shelves of potions and leather-bound books lined the walls. Also fixed to the walls were wide wooden counters, upon which lay various knives and other metal utensils. Two young women were chained in one corner, both on the floor, unconscious.

Focus, Mona. You don't have much time.

Averting my eyes away from them, I approached one of the shelves. Heaving off a thick black book, I placed it down on the counter. I flipped through the fading parchment pages until I reached the recipe I needed.

My breath hitched as I looked at the complexity of it. I looked around the ingredients shelves and prayed that we had everything.

I approached one of the cauldrons in the center of the room and stoked a fire. I ran around the room, collecting bottles off the shelves and tipping them into the black pot. Fortunately, we did have everything. Arielle always made sure that we were well stocked.

The cauldron bubbled and spluttered as I churned it. An hour later, it had formed into a thick orange liquid. I sniffed it, worrying that I might have burnt it.

I scraped it out of the cauldron and poured it into a metal goblet. Then I cleaned up, leaving the room in the state that I'd found it.

Concealing the goblet with my cloak, I climbed out of the spell room and closed the trapdoor behind me.

Then I transported myself back to Rhys' chambers to check if he had returned yet. Relieved to see that he hadn't, I walked straight out of the room and toward Kiev's apartment. I ducked down in the shadows in the far end of his corridor and waited.

It was ten o'clock and Tiarni still hadn't shown up, so I could only assume that Kiev had gotten her in there before I had arrived. Either that, or he'd failed to lure her in.

I walked over to his door and placed my ear against the door.

Soft moaning.

She's in there.

I opened the door and stepped inside, closing the door behind me as quietly as I could.

I crept along the hallway and peeked through the bedroom door, which had been left open.

I felt a sharp twinge in my chest as I caught sight of the redhead lying beneath Kiev in his bed. Although they were still clothed, the way he was touching her cut me deep. Swallowing back the pain, I ducked down on the floor and crawled until I was as close as possible to where they were lying.

I raised my head up to the bed's level. Tiarni's eyes were closed as Kiev kissed her, but he noticed me. I held up the goblet. He seemed to understand.

"Close your eyes," he whispered into Tiarni's ear, his voice hoarse and seductive.

"Why?"

"It's a surprise."

"Okay," she breathed.

He kept one hand over her eyes while he reached the other hand out to me. I passed him the goblet.

"Open your mouth."

Tiarni did as she was told and Kiev tipped the liquid down her throat. She coughed and spluttered.

"Wha-what are you…"

Her voice trailed off as the liquid began to take effect.

Kiev crawled off of her and stood next to me as we both stared down at her. Her eyeballs rolled in their sockets and her whole body trembled. As soon as her lips began to swell, I gripped her head between my hands and closed my eyes, picturing the visions that I was about to implant in her as memories.

The night the humans escaped The Shade, you let them out. You also let the humans free on your own island. You did this to take revenge on Rhys for shunning you all these years in favor of Mona who is nothing but a traitor. You've never forgiven him for it. You knew how important his and Isolde's rituals are to him right now, so you wanted to disrupt them. While you were freeing the humans on your own island, Celice followed you and tried to stop you. You killed her and dumped her body in the sea.

I let go of her.

She stopped trembling and her eyelids flickered shut.

I swallowed back the lump in my throat and looked up at Kiev.

"There's no ritual tonight," I croaked. "She needs to stay with you now until morning. By about nine o'clock, she will wake up with the memories I implanted in her... and her confession will force out of her lips when Rhys interrogates her."

"What confession?"

"You'll see."

My hands trembling, I rushed out of the room.

Tiarni always had gone out of her way to make my life hell, but I knew the kind of punishment that would befall her now. A punishment that even she could never deserve.

But it was done now. I'd made my decision. I'd taken it upon myself to sacrifice her life in favor of ours. It was too late for regrets or second thoughts.

Two murders. In the space of a few days.

Who will be next?

Chapter 6: Kiev

Mona is darker than I imagined.

I still didn't understand what fate would befall Tiarni or even what she would confess to Rhys, but I knew enough about the warlock by now to know that he wouldn't let her off lightly.

As Mona had predicted, Tiarni woke up at about nine o'clock. She looked up at me and smiled seductively. She clearly didn't remember anything about Mona interrupting us.

"Good morning, Kiev."

I kept Tiarni occupied in my room until I heard a knock at the door. I opened it to see Efren, her ginger brother, standing there.

"Rhys wants to see you both now."

I walked back into the bedroom.

"It's your brother," I said. "Get dressed."

"Why?"

"Rhys needs to talk to us."

Panic filled her eyes. I picked up her gown from the floor and helped her get into it. Catching her by the hand, I led her out of the room, hoping Efren wouldn't detect anything strange about her behavior as we walked. Thankfully, he walked ahead of us so he didn't.

The more we neared the dining hall, the more Tiarni dragged her feet. I picked her up and carried her the rest of the way. I put her down once we arrived outside the entrance.

Efren glanced at his sister just before we entered. "You look so pale." He frowned, lifting a hand to her cheek. "It's nothing to worry about, Tiarni. It's just Rhys and I going through procedure."

Afraid at what he was seeing in her, I tugged on Tiarni's arm and pulled her into the room. Rhys sat at the end of the long table, leaning back in his chair, one boot resting on the seat next to him.

He remained silent, watching us as we each pulled up a chair.

Once we were sitting, he cleared his throat.

His eyes settled on me first.

"Novalic, I admit that I barely know you, but your siblings have been loyal to us for many years now." He picked up a quill and placed it down on a piece of parchment. "Tell me, where were you the night the humans—"

"I did it," Tiarni blurted out. Her knuckles were white as she clenched her fists together on the table, her nostrils flaring as she began to take in shallow breaths. "I freed the humans."

Efren's jaw dropped.

Rhys was also stunned into silence, his lips parting as he stared at her.

"Tiarni," Efren gasped. "What are you saying?"

"I did it. I set all the humans free, both on this island and also back home!"

"Why would you do that?" Rhys spoke this time, his voice low and menacing.

"Because of you!" Tiarni screamed, jumping up from her seat and walking over to Rhys, glaring down at him. "All I've ever wanted is for you to return my love. But every time, you turned me away for that scrawny blonde. Even Kiev I only slept with hoping to make you jealous!" She sank to her knees and began sobbing. "I've taken your insults for too long, Rhys. I needed to do something to soothe the wounds you've caused me."

Rhys stood up, towering over her, his chest heaving.

Efren jumped up and placed his hand over Tiarni's forehead. He looked up at Rhys with desperate eyes.

"Can't you see she's sick? Rhys, listen to me. There's no way in hell my sister would have done this." He turned to face Tiarni and shook her. "What are you saying? Of course you didn't do this."

In two strides Rhys had walked over and pulled Efren away from his sister. He reached for her ear and twisted it until she yelped in pain.

"Once and for all, I will punish you for this stubborn infatuation you have with me." He threw her down, her head bashing against the stone floor.

Rhys picked up his pen and parchment and, glaring at Efren, said, "This investigation is over."

He reached back down to pick up Tiarni. He caught hold of her long hair and pulled her into a standing position.

Tears streamed down her cheeks and her lips quivered as she breathed, "I-I also murdered Celice."

A stunned silence fell upon the hall.

"Celice followed me back home," Tiarni cried. "I killed her and dropped her body in the sea. R-Rhys, I only did it because—"

Efren yelled and gripped Tiarni by the throat, choking her before she could utter another incriminating word.

But it was too late.

Rhys burned with a fury so wild, I could practically feel his blood boiling. Tiarni screamed as he pounced on her, and they both vanished.

Chapter 7: Mona

All the residents of the island gathered that night on the beach. We stood around a heap of wood. Rhys had insisted on building the pyre himself.

Julisse and Arielle had scanned the island in search of Celice one last time at the plea of Efren, just to check that Celice definitely wasn't here and this wasn't all just a strange lie by Tiarni. Of course, they'd returned unsuccessful.

Now Rhys prepared the wood, his face white. He walked over to Tiarni, who lay semi-conscious on the ground a few feet away. Now, he wanted her to be fully conscious again.

Rhys had already pried away her fingernails and toenails one by one with a blunt knife. Then he'd torn away her hair with his bare fists, until her scalp was a patchy, bloody mess.

We had all watched, as was our custom whenever a traitor was found among us. Even Efren had been forced to stand by. I looked at the scattered nails and hair on the sand a few meters away.

Now, Rhys stripped Tiarni naked and threw her clothes on the pyre.

"No!" she shrieked, coming to consciousness again and clutching Rhys' shirt. "Please don't do this. Rhys, I love you! I love you! I've always loved you—"

"Silence!"

Rhys struck her with his fist so hard I was sure he'd broken her jaw.

He tied her against the post erected in the center of the wood, fixing her there with magic bonds that no amount of struggling could break free from.

I looked at Efren. He had averted his eyes to the ground, tears spilling down his cheeks.

A spark emanated from Rhys' palm and a fierce bonfire erupted. We all took a step back from the sudden heat.

Tiarni's bloodcurdling screams filled the night air.

Rhys resumed his place next to me, his jaw clenched, his hollow black eyes flickering against the flames.

I felt like I was about to throw up. My stomach had twisted itself into knots so tight I could barely breathe.

I should be the one burning in that fire right now. And yet I decided to save my life at the cost of an innocent's.

How could I have done this?

What is happening to me?

I held my hands against my ears as the flames licked Tiarni's skin and melted her through to the bone.

I choked on the smoke as it stung my eyes. The smell of burnt flesh pervaded the area—a stench that even the sea breeze was having trouble dissipating.

Julisse and Arielle stood on the other side of Rhys, sobbing in each other's arms. Isolde, their aunt, who stood still further along, had an expression almost as controlled as Rhys.

Rhys' face was still ashen, his eyes still fixed on the fire.

Sensing my gaze on him, he muttered, "And this is what we do to traitors."

I shivered.

I feared that Rhys' darkness had penetrated my being too much already. Without me even realizing it.

As I looked back at the flames that had now devoured the young redhead, one thought circled in my mind:

I need to get away from this life.

Chapter 8: Kiev

I had never cared for the redhead, but I wouldn't have wished such a fate upon her.

The crowd finally dispersed as the bonfire began to dim. Rhys turned to Efren before leaving and pointed to the heap of his sister's nails and hair on the sand. "Burn those too," he said.

Efren glared after Rhys as he walked away. It looked like it was all he could do to stop himself from attacking Rhys.

I had looked over at Mona from across the bonfire several times throughout the burning. Her expression had been hard to read. I still couldn't shake the surprise over what she had done. Even I wouldn't have been so quick to condemn Tiarni to such a fate.

I waited for the hushed crowds to leave, and I avoided joining my siblings even though they beckoned me over. I told them that I would stay outside a while longer.

That left just Efren and I. He bent down over the remains of his sister.

"Novalic," he rasped.

He stood up, a bunch of curly red hair clutched in his pale hand.

"You spent much time with my sister during her last days." He squinted at me through the thick grey smoke. "You know that she didn't do this."

I took a deep breath, unsure of how to respond.

"Was she not sharing your bed the nights these humans and Celice disappeared?"

"Evidently not," I said coldly.

The accusatory tone of his voice put me on edge.

Brushing away sweat from his forehead with the back of his sleeve, he staggered a few steps toward me.

"This was all so unlike her," he said softly. "Yes, she loved Rhys, but she never would have done something so foolish. She valued her life more than this." He held up the clump of hair. "Wouldn't you agree?"

I took a step away from him and started walking toward the woods.

"Wait."

I turned around slowly to face him again.

He narrowed his eyes on me.

"I know you have something to do with this. Why else would she behave the way she did? You did something to her that made her get this insane idea into her head. Maybe she did even murder Celice and let all the humans free. But there had to be some other incentive than taking vengeance on Rhys. An incentive that only came about once she started seeing you…"

I glared back at him.

"Careful, warlock," I said. "I would think long and hard before making accusations of me."

He backed down.

But as I left, I felt his eyes follow me.

Chapter 9: Mona

Rhys left early the next morning to look for his sister's body. He hoped that they would be able to give her a proper funeral. He thought perhaps the corpse might have washed up along the shore of our island. When he returned a few hours later unsuccessful, he concluded that it must have floated too far already, or been eaten by a shark.

All rituals were cancelled for three days as the siblings mourned the loss of Celice. The first two days Rhys didn't exchange a word even with me. He, Julisse and Arielle locked themselves up in the spell room. But by the third night, Rhys returned to our bedroom just before midnight.

I shivered as his body brushed against mine, his arm reaching over my waist as he rested his chin on my bare shoulder.

His breathing became heavier as he fell asleep.

I felt sick beneath his touch. The weight of his strong arm pressing against my stomach made me want to throw up. Adding more pressure than I was already bearing from murdering two young women.

I reached for his hand and slid out from underneath him, walking over to the balcony.

I looked back at Rhys' face. I did this sometimes when he was sleeping to detect in him any traces of the person he used to be.

He was frowning, his lips tight, as if in pain. It was an expression I seldom saw in him when he was awake. It reminded me of when he was a boy. My best friend. I'd known all his expressions so well then and I still kept them treasured in my memory.

Another pang of guilt hit me.

I remembered the agony of losing my own family. I didn't wish that pain on Rhys. And yet I had caused it so carelessly.

"I'm sorry," I breathed.

I walked back over to the bed and brushed away his wavy dark hair from his face, placing a gentle kiss on his forehead. He stirred and opened his eyes. He reached for me and wrapped his arms around me, pulling me beneath the covers. I rested my head against his chest, listening to his heartbeat. Even though it cut me to think of the suffering he was going through, the fact that he could still experience pain and loss brought me comfort. When he was awake, he concealed his feelings so well that I'd believed he didn't have them.

"I'm sorry," I repeated, louder this time.

He grunted and rolled over on his side, his back facing me.

I broke down into tears.

"I'm so sorry you lost your sister."

Sobs racked my body as all the tension built up over the last few days flooded out. I reached my arm around him and pressed my wet cheek against his back. He tensed beneath my touch. Then he turned back around to face me. He sat up in bed, looking down at me.

"It's been a heavy loss," he said, his voice hoarse, as he brushed away my tears with his thumb. "But you ought not to cry over it. I told Julisse and Arielle the same. It may be difficult to bear now, but we must see it as a test to make us all stronger."

I shouldn't have expected his response to be any different. Rhys always did see everything that happened in life in light of the Cause. Even the death of his own sister.

Neither of us slept that night. His hands ran through my hair absentmindedly as I lay against him. It was hard to relax beneath his touch after the night's events. I shivered as I thought about the strength of those hands. How they had ripped Tiarni's hair from her skull. Those hands that now caressed me so gently would have treated me just as they had Tiarni had he known that I was the cause of his sister's death.

***

Rhys rose early, took a shower and dressed.

"Things will return to normal now that we have caught the traitor," he said, fastening a cloak around him. "We have wasted too much time already. Isolde was so close to making a breakthrough."

I didn't know what this breakthrough was, but I dared not ask. I feared the answer.

"I don't sense that you're particularly bothered our rituals have been delayed," he said, eyeing me as I lay in bed.

I rubbed my head in my hands and sighed. The last thing I wanted right now was one of Rhys' tirades about how I didn't share the same passion as him for our ancestors' cause.

"I'm just... tired, Rhys. It's been a difficult few days."

He crossed his arms over his chest and stared down at me.

I groaned internally. He was going to take out his frustration on me. I knew Rhys better than he knew himself sometimes.

Even though he seemed to believe that he was above experiencing emotions, he wasn't. They just built up and manifested themselves in different ways. And I was normally the one to bear the brunt of his mood swings.

I stood up.

"You're right," I muttered. "I don't share the same enthusiasm as you for these rituals."

"I've warned you before. If you don't align yourself with the will of our Ancients as the rest of us do, sooner or later you'll fall into trouble again. And this time, I won't be able to make any more exceptions for you." He walked over to me and gripped my shoulders. "Don't you trust me? Is that what this is? After all we've been through together, you still can't surrender?"

I stared into his intense black eyes. It felt like I already had lost myself to him.

"You know that I can make you as powerful as me. I can make you a Channeler," he breathed, his mouth inches away from my ear. "Remember what I've always told you, Mona. With surrender comes freedom. If you'd just let me show you…"

He let go of me and stormed out. The room shook as he slammed the door shut behind him.

But his last words echoed around in my head long after he'd left our apartment.

"With surrender comes freedom."

Maybe that's what I have to do.

Maybe the only way out of this darkness is to first plunge myself further into it.

Maybe I have to be lost in order to be found.

Chapter 10: Kiev

"I'm sorry I doubted you about those humans." Helina sat perched on the edge of her bed.

Erik was leaning against the edge of the small table in the corner of her bedroom, while I was seated in a chair in the corner of the room.

"I was just so fearful," she continued. "We can't lose you again, Kiev."

I stared at my siblings. It still felt strange to be in their presence. Although they were so familiar to me, they were also like strangers.

I got up and walked over to Helina, planting a kiss on her forehead. I wanted to promise her that she wouldn't lose me again. After everything they'd been through without me, I owed them that much. But I couldn't. Just as I wasn't able to promise Mona that anything would work out between us. Because I didn't know. Especially now.

"I suppose you understand now why it's not a good idea to mess with Rhys," Erik said dryly.

I remained silent.

"There's something else I should have mentioned earlier," Erik continued. "Around the back of this building is a trapdoor. None of us are supposed to even know it exists, but I caught Julisse coming out of it one day. Anyway, it's an underground chamber. The witches' spell room. Never go in there, no matter what."

I raised a brow.

"Once a vampire goes in there, he doesn't come out. Only witches are allowed in a spell room. If any other creature goes in there, the power of the room diminishes. All these years of building up the room's potency, gone for nothing. The only way to prevent this waste is to sacrifice the person who's stepped inside."

"Sacrifice?"

Erik nodded grimly. "I don't know what they'd do because we've never witnessed it. But just... stay away from that damn room, will you?"

"Promise, Kiev," Helina said, tugging on my arm.

"All right. I'll stay away."

We all fell silent. The image of Tiarni burning alive at the stake was still fresh in our minds. Erik heaved a sigh and sat down in a chair.

"I'm sorry, Kiev," he muttered.

"What?"

"I'm sorry that you're in this situation because of us. I know it's far from ideal."

His words surprised me.

"What situation?"

"Being here… on this island. Bound to serve the witches."

"Why would you apologize? I thought you were just telling me recently how great life here is, you two being Lord and Lady of this place."

His shoulders sagged and he rested his forehead in his hand.

"You know it's not," Helina said quietly. "I guess believing that life is better here helps us cope."

"Well, if there's anything you should be sorry for," I said, my voice rising, "it's chasing away Matteo and making it look like I set him up."

My blood boiled just recalling what they'd done, the look in Matteo's eyes as he boarded his ship. I still hadn't forgiven them for what they'd done. I wasn't sure that I ever could.

"We're sorry for that too," Erik said.

Helina placed a hand on my arm. "But we had to do it. It would have been too dangerous for you to stay on the island otherwise. If Rhys had found out you had ties with

Matteo…" She gulped.

I brushed her away from me.

"You could have told me that. I could have broken things off with Matteo myself. There was no excuse for what you did."

Neither argued back. Their heads hung.

I placed my head in my hands, trying to stop recalling that painful day. I remained quiet for several minutes as I reeled in my temper.

"It's done now," I said eventually.

I walked out of the room, leaving them in their guilty silence, and exited my sister's apartment.

On returning to my own apartment, I was surprised to see Mona waiting for me in my bedroom. Her hair was tied back in a tight bun, and she wore a high-necked black dress that touched the floor.

She looked paler than ever. Her lips trembled as she opened her mouth to speak.

"I can't see you any more."

I stopped walking toward her as a tear spilled down her cheek.

"We've covered our tracks. And now I can't keep seeing you behind Rhys' back. I don't want to be responsible for throwing another person into the fire."

I remained silent, my eyes fixed on hers.

"And I can't keep living in between two men like this. I

don't even know what we had to begin with, but whatever it was…" She swallowed hard and looked down at the floor. "It's over, Kiev."

Chapter 11: Mona

I wasn't sure that I'd ever be able to get that vampire out of my subconscious. But I knew that I had to try, or I would fail to become powerful enough to break free from Rhys. To become a true Channeler of our Ancients.

I just have to hope that I make it out the other end.

I waited until after that night's ritual to tell Rhys. As we crossed the courtyard heading back to our room, I gripped his arm and tugged him to a stop. He looked at me questioningly. I led him to the fountain and stopped in front of it.

I slipped both of my hands into his. Looking down at the ground, I cleared my throat.

"I've been thinking about what you said." My voice

trembled as I spoke. "I'll do it. I'll stop resisting."

His black eyes bored into me. His thumb reached beneath my chin and pushed my head up so that I was forced to face him.

"You know what this means, right?"

I nodded, my throat drying out.

"Why do you want this?"

"I want to stop living my life in limbo," I whispered, shutting my eyes.

It's too painful.

He breathed out. "I've been telling you to take this leap since the beginning. What's made you decide now?"

"Because I want to be yours, Rhys. I know we are bonded, but that doesn't make me truly yours until I've become like you."

"Why do you want me now? What's changed since you returned to me?"

I bit my lip.

"I'm not sure. I just know something has changed." I winced at how unconvincing I sounded.

He crossed his arms over his chest, frowning at me.

"Mona, I have to be sure you really are ready for this. Because once we start, there's no going back. You either complete this successfully and gain the ability to channel our Ancients' power, or you break."

"I-I understand," I stammered.

He stared at me long and hard. Then he took my hand and transported us back to our bedroom.

"Sit down," he ordered.

I sat on the bed.

He bent down to my level and gripped my jaw. "You're fearful," he said. "That's not a good first sign."

I bit my lip.

"This fear must go. You need to welcome this challenge with open arms, not fearing it."

He stood up abruptly.

"Get up."

"What?"

"Walk over to the balcony."

I stared at him, confused. He glared and pointed to the open balcony doors.

"Stand up on the balcony railing. But do not use magic to balance yourself."

I eyed the railing.

"There's no way I can balance myself on that without magic."

"Just do it."

I threw him another glance before making my way over to the balcony. I looked over the edge. Then I wished I hadn't reminded myself how many hundreds of feet we were above ground.

I gripped the railing. Chills ran across my skin.

"There's no way I can do this without magic," I repeated.

He walked onto the balcony and stood next to me.

"Do you think I would ask you to do this if I thought you incapable of it? Do you think I want to murder you?"

I don't know.

"No," I muttered.

Keeping my eyes away from the steep drop, I lifted one shaking foot onto the ledge and tried to balance before raising the other one.

This is impossible.

I held onto one of the balcony pillars as both feet were now balancing on the railing.

"Now let go of the pillar."

My heart hammered against my chest.

There's no way I can do this.

Closing my eyes, I chanted a balancing charm in my mind, hoping that Rhys wouldn't notice I was using magic.

I let go, pretending to flail my arms about as I balanced perfectly.

As I moved away from the column and walked to the center, the spell lifted. A gust of wind blew against me, making me lose my footing. Gravity sucked me downward, and the wind rushed past me as I hurtled toward the ground.

I tried to scream out a levitation charm but it didn't have any effect. My powers seemed to have completely drained out of me. My eyes watered from the wind and I closed my eyes, preparing for the impact.

I expected my body to shatter, but instead, I found myself being caught by two strong arms, my body parallel with the ground, about three feet away from it. Rhys was levitating above me.

He lowered me gently to the ground, then pulled me upright.

My knees crumpled and I curled up on the floor, shaking.

"I told you not to use magic," Rhys said.

"I would have fallen even faster had I not," I gasped, glaring up at him.

"That's not the point," he said calmly. "I told you not to use it. If you want to succeed at this, you need to follow my instructions blindly. You are not to consider the consequences." He bent down closer to me, brushing the hair away from my face. "Your only duty is to trust me."

I continued to shake.

"Clearly, you still have not understood this. You need more practice. Tomorrow, we'll give you just that."

More practice.

His words plagued me as I lay in bed that night.

Chapter 12: Mona

Rhys made us leave our apartment early the next morning. We stopped outside his aunt Isolde's door a few meters along from ours.

The witch came to the door after a few knocks, wearing a woolen night gown, her long grey-streaked hair tied up above her head in a bun.

"Mona and I will be leaving for a while," Rhys said. "I'm not sure when we'll return. So go on with the rituals without us."

Isolde pursed her lips as her cold eyes settled on me.

"Where are you going?"

Rhys glanced down at me, then looked back at his aunt.

"Mona has decided to become a Channeler."

She raised her eyebrows, eyeing me.

"Does she understand what that involves?"

"She will soon," Rhys said.

"Very well." Isolde closed her door.

Rhys gripped my arm and led me further along the corridor.

"When are you going to give me my magic back?" I asked irritably.

"Not yet."

"What's that supposed to mean?"

He stopped short and glared down at me.

"You'll see."

He reached out suddenly and held both of my hands in his. We vanished from the spot.

Several seconds later, I felt sand beneath my feet. I opened my eyes and as the scene around me came into focus, my heart skipped a beat.

"The ogres' island," I gasped, gripping Rhys' arm so hard the blood drained from my knuckles.

It felt like I was living a nightmare as I stared up at the black metal gate that towered over us, its spikes topped with human heads. "I can't be here! If they find me—"

"They'll break your bones one by one and then skin you alive. I know. You murdered the king's son."

"They why are we here? Are you insane?"

Rhys remained calm. "Do you trust me?"

I stared at him disbelievingly.

"Trust you to what?"

"To hold your life in the palm of my hand."

I paused.

"You already do," I whispered.

"No. You have a choice. I can give you back your magic and we can return to the island. You don't have to do this."

I looked again at the dark silhouette of those gates, shuddering at the screams that seemed to pierce through the mountains themselves. The smell of roasting flesh drifted over the kingdom's high walls, being carried by the sea breeze. It was lunch time.

But I do have to do this. I don't have a choice.

I looked up at him again. His eyes remained fixed intensely on my face, as if studying my every emotion.

"I-I'll do it."

"That's not what I asked you."

"I... trust you."

"Are you afraid?"

I bit my lower lip to stop it trembling.

"If you really trust me, you won't be afraid."

"I'm not afraid."

He ran a hand through my hair, brushing away the stray strands from my face and tucking them behind my ear.

"Hm," he muttered. "We'll see about that."

He gripped my arm again and began marching me full

speed toward the skull-topped gates. With each step we took, my knees felt weaker.

He stopped a few feet away from it and let go of me.

"Now you will knock on this gate, and wait until they answer."

I was sure that I would have a heart attack before the ogres ever opened the gate.

"Wh-what will you do?"

"What I may or may not do doesn't concern you. Just do as I say."

What if they snap me in two the moment they lay eyes on me and Rhys doesn't even have a chance to intervene?

He turned on his heel and began walking away in the opposite direction, toward the sea.

I looked after him desperately.

"Wait!" I croaked. "You're not even going to give me a knife?"

He glared back at me over his shoulder. That was all the answer I needed.

Blind surrender. That's what Rhys demands of me.

I turned back to face the gates again. My knees were shaking so much, it was a struggle to support my own weight.

Even though I felt insane, I closed the distance between myself and the gates. Picking up a rock from the ground, I slammed it with all the strength I could muster against the metal. The stone hitting the iron gave off an eerie rattle.

I took a step back and listened.

A deafening crack pierced through the air as the gate unbolted. Then there was a creak as the gates opened. I whirled around and scanned the shoreline for Rhys. He had vanished. On turning back to face the gate, I found myself standing in full view of a giant ogre. His tusks were stained with grease, and he held some kind of roasted limb in one arm. I had disturbed his lunch.

His mouth dropped open. I was sure that he recognized me. I supposed that the whole kingdom would have been put on alert for me.

"You dare show your face around here?" he boomed.

I stood rooted to the spot.

I didn't struggle as he hurled me over his shoulder and retreated with me behind the gates. I closed my eyes, trying to block out the terror and focus on Rhys' words. His calm face. His steady breathing.

"Do you trust me?"

I'd said yes. Now more than ever, I needed that to be true.

Even as the gate clanged shut behind us, I kept thinking of Rhys. He was the only thing I had to cling to to keep my sanity.

I didn't open my eyes even when the ogre slammed me down against a cold floor.

"It's the killer! I have her!" the ogre bellowed above me.

His shouts echoed around me. We must have been inside the mountain already. Still I didn't open my eyes.

Rough hands picked me up and dragged me across the floor.

"She's here!"

Footsteps approached.

Hands closed around my neck. I gasped in pain as I was lifted off the floor, my windpipe being crushed. Still, I dared not open my eyes. Rhys hadn't even offered me a reassurance. He'd simply asked me a question. It was up to me to decide whether he deserved my trust.

A blade sliced against my cheek. Blood trickled down toward my neck. And then it sliced again, this time deeper, cutting right through my lower lip.

I gripped the coarse hands around my neck, trying to loosen them to let me gasp for air.

My back was slammed against a cold wall. My head bashed against it, adding to my dizziness. Still, I kept my eyes shut.

They talked amongst themselves but I was in too much pain to make sense of their words.

"Open your eyes," one of them shouted.

I kept them shut. If I opened them I would lose myself to fear completely.

Cold fingers forced my eyes open. I found myself face to face with an ogre quite different from the guard who'd met me by the gate. Her features were sharper and more regal, her body more shapely. I recognized her as the queen of this place.

"Now, hold her eyes in place," she said, looking up at one of the ogre guards towering over me.

He held my eyelids open. I watched in horror as she reached for her belt and withdrew a long knife.

"You know what this is, girl?" She glared at me. "A carving knife. Watch as I prepare you for my meal tonight."

Another ogre held me down as I began to struggle. The queen reached for my hand and stretched out my arm. As she grazed the knife over my skin, a grin split her face.

"Mmm. I'm going to enjoy this." She looked up at a tall, slim ogre I recognized as her king. "Make sure you watch every second of this, darling."

Rhys, where are you?

Any sliver of faith I might have had in him was evaporating by the second.

Why would he leave it this late if he still intended to rescue me?

She ran her hands along my right arm until she reached my middle finger. I let out a scream as she broke it with one sharp motion.

Maybe Rhys wanted to get rid of me after all. Maybe he found out about Kiev and this is his revenge.

I thought again of Tiarni, and how I'd been forced to

watch as he'd pried away her fingernails one by one.

He is sick enough to do this to me.

My thoughts were ludicrous. There was no way Rhys could have found out. But all ability to think was slipping away from me.

The queen moved onto my index finger. Another crack filled the dark hall as she snapped that one too. Darkness clouded my vision. I was close to passing out. The guard behind me slapped my face.

"No drifting off to sleep." The queen glared up at me. "We've only just begun. If you stay awake long enough, and if I sever you in just the right places, you might even last until the frying."

Grinning, she moved on to my third finger.

Then she shrieked and scrambled back away from me, dropping her knife on the floor as though she'd been burnt. The ogres holding me in place let go at the same time. My eyes rolled as I tried to make sense of what was happening.

There came a sudden gush of wind, and then I was lying in sand. I blinked and sat up. I was back on the beach outside the gates, with Rhys staring down at me.

I swore beneath my breath, cradling my broken hand against my chest. Tears of pain streamed down my face.

"How did it feel when you thought that I might not come for me?"

How do you think it felt, you bastard? I wanted to yell at him, but I felt barely strong enough to whisper. I closed my eyes and winced, biting my lip against the pain.

"It was crushing, wasn't it?"

"What was the point of all that?" I gasped. "Why didn't you come for me before the bitch broke my fingers?" I groaned.

"Now, you won't forget how doubting me is associated with pain. It's not a nice feeling. And you won't want to feel it again."

This man is insane.

"I don't understand." A fresh bout of pain shot through my arm, lighting my nerves on fire.

He bent down and unclasped my injured hand from my chest. He cupped my hand between his. A few seconds later, the pain was gone. I flexed my fingers. They moved as if nothing had happened. Then Rhys ran a finger along my cheek and lower lip. The wounds stung as he touched them, and my skin became smooth. He held out his hand and pulled me to my feet, gripping me by the waist to steady me.

"Physical pain comes and goes," he said. "It's inconsequential. A means to an end. But the mental pain you experienced will remain with you forever. I don't think you'll ever forget what just went on in there."

You don't say.

He began guiding me toward the edge of the ocean.

"Where are you taking me now?" I asked irritably.

"Now, I want you to feel what it's like to not doubt me."

Chapter 13: Mona

We reappeared in a pitch-black forest. The sound of rain on the canopy of leaves above was deafening, although the broad-leaved trees offered some shelter.

"Where are—"

I caught sight of Rhys slipping behind the trunk of a tree.

"Rhys?" I motioned to follow him.

"No, stay where you are," he whispered back. "I'll be right here."

A howl pierced the night air. There was a rustling about ten feet away from me in the bushes, and the sound of sniffing. A few moments later, a massive black wolf bounded into the clearing. Its orange eyes glared at me as it bared its fangs.

"Over here," the wolf growled.

A werewolf. But this beast was larger and more fierce than any werewolf I'd ever seen before.

There was more rustling in the bushes and half a dozen more wolves entered the clearing—all just as huge.

"What is it?"

One of the wolves began to approach closer, sniffing the air to catch my scent.

"A witch." A deep voice spoke from behind me.

I turned around to see Rhys walking out from one of the trees.

"You," the wolf hissed, glaring at Rhys.

"He's the one I saw by the mountain," a second wolf growled. "He took Isiah and her pack."

We're kidnapping werewolves now? When will it end?

"Yes, that's me," Rhys said calmly.

"I'd suggest you leave now," the wolf snarled. "Unless you enjoy the feeling of the flesh being sucked from your bones."

"Your witch, on the other hand," another wolf said, "can stay as long as she likes." Its mouth salivated as it looked at me.

The werewolves began to close in around us. Rhys gripped my shoulder.

"Stay back," he muttered.

He pushed me to the ground behind him just as the leader of the pack leapt toward us, its weight causing the ground to shake. As soon as I touched the leaves, a forcefield shot up around me.

My breathing quickened as two werewolves leapt toward me, only to be propelled back by Rhys' barrier.

I didn't know why Rhys didn't just use one of his powerful curses to finish the lot in one swoop. Instead he withdrew a long silver dagger from his belt.

Maybe he wants to put on a show for me.

As the leader hurtled toward him, he dodged the creature's jaws and swung himself up onto its back.

With one sharp motion, he stabbed the werewolf in the neck. The werewolf collapsed and Rhys jumped off.

"Who's next?" Rhys' growl sounded just as fierce as the werewolves'.

Another wolf leapt at him. Rhys dodged again and, spinning round, sliced through the animal's back leg. The wolf howled in agony and collapsed, writhing on the floor as blood soaked the ground.

The other wolves now looked more hesitant to approach.

"What's wrong? You can't handle fighting me man to man? I'm not even using magic on you."

His words incensed the werewolves who remained standing enough that three of them leapt forward at once. I gasped as one of them pinned Rhys to the ground, knocking his dagger out of his hand. Lowering its head to Rhys' face, the beast stretched out its jaws. Rhys lifted his leg and kicked the wolf hard in its underbelly, hard enough to make the giant animal groan and loosen its grip for a second. That was all the opportunity Rhys needed to stab the wolf in the eye with his finger.

The wolf howled. It lowered its head to bite him again. Rhys caught its jaws just before they closed down on him and, though its sharp teeth must have been cutting through Rhys' fingers, he pushed upward, jerking the wolf's head back, and managed to reach for its second eye.

The wolf rolled off of him onto its back and thrashed about on the ground. Rhys got to his feet and glared around at the remaining wolves. They stared back at him, then backed away. Although they were clearly loath to, they didn't see it as worth losing their lives or their limbs over Rhys.

Or perhaps they were just planning to return with reinforcements.

Once they'd all disappeared, Rhys finally used his magic again. He manifested a rope and tied the three werewolves lying on the floor together by their front legs. Then he grabbed the other end of it and approached me, dragging their tremendous weight along with him. His chest was heaving as he wiped his forehead with his sleeve and brushed away the black curls that framed his face.

He touched the protective boundary surrounding me and it disappeared just as suddenly as it had formed.

He held out his hand and I gripped it. He pulled me to

my feet. I couldn't stop staring at him. I'd known how powerful he was with magic. And I'd known that he was physically strong without it. But I'd had no idea that he was strong enough to tackle werewolves with his bare hands and barely break a sweat. *This is vampire-level strength.* I'd never seen any witch display such prowess without the use of magic.

Rhys walked over to his dagger and, wiping the blood off it with the hem of his cloak, slid it back into its sheath in his belt.

Still holding the end of the rope attached to the suffering wolves, he walked back over to me and held my hand.

He looked down at me through his thick dark lashes, still breathing deeply from the fight.

And then, before I could stop him, he reached for the back of my neck and pulled me against him, hungrily claiming my lips. He kissed me with a passion that I'd rarely experienced in him. His right hand hiked up my dress and rested on my inner thigh, the black rose etched in my skin prickling beneath his touch.

I was speechless as our lips parted. Raindrops dripped from his dark hair onto my cheeks as he stared down at me, his eyes burning with need.

"I love you, Mona."

This man is going to be the ruin of me.

Chapter 14: Mona

Rhys transported us back not back to The Shade, but to our own island. As we appeared outside the main door of the castle, I almost screamed in fright as I laid eyes on the beasts he'd brought along with us.

Rhys took the werewolves down to one of the dungeons. I made my way up to our chambers at the top of the castle. He reappeared a few minutes later carrying a tray containing a jug of dark red blood and two wine glasses. I stared at the tray in disgust, daring to believe that this was werewolf blood.

He placed the tray down in the living room. We both changed into dry clothes and then sat by the fire.

I hadn't said anything to him since he'd kissed me. I

wasn't sure what to say any more.

I understood that he was trying to train me to channel the power of our Ancients. My mind couldn't be resistant to him. But I didn't understand how loving me was mixed in with all of this. Rhys never was one to mix in his personal feelings with tasks in service of our ancestors. But now I found myself doubting his true motivation.

Is he just trying to train me, or is he also trying to win my heart?

Rhys sat back in his chair, his eyes fixed on the crackling fire.

I cleared my throat.

"So, what's next?"

Rhys continued to stare at the fireplace, his irises glimmering in the flickering light.

He replied only after several minutes. "I want you to be safe for what is to come," he said, his voice deep. "Most witches lose their minds before they even come close to succeeding."

Although I'd heard about how difficult it was to become a Channeler, I'd never understood what was involved. Rhys, Julisse, Arielle and Isolde were the only Channelers among us.

Rhys glanced at me briefly before returning his gaze to the fire. "It helps," he continued, "to have something to cling to. *Someone* to cling to. To place your faith in. Without that, you feel like you're lost in oblivion. Holding onto sanity is like trying to grasp hold of sand even as it slips between your fingers… I remember what it was like."

I felt more and more uneasy with each word.

"Most witches get lost and never find themselves again," he continued. "They lose their ability to feel anything but pain and paranoia."

I wondered then if Rhys was one of these people. Sometimes his passion and desire were almost tangible—like when he'd kissed me in the rain a few hours ago. Other times, he felt distant. Although he proclaimed love to me, I didn't know if he was just remembering what he'd felt for me before he became a Channeler.

"So, uh, you had Isolde to keep your faith in?"

The shadow of a smile crossed his face.

"Yes. I had my aunt. That's how I pulled through. But even then, it was difficult beyond measure." He turned to face me again. "But you see, the stronger the bond is, the easier it will be. Being Isolde's nephew, I have a natural bond with her. But it's obviously not the same as… a lover, for example. It would have been easier had I had that."

I averted my eyes to the floor, feeling uncomfortable beneath his gaze.

"Of course, you are already bonded to me," he went on. "Physically. But mentally, I know you're still not. And that is what will cause you problems once the process starts. I can guide you through this, but only if your mind becomes one with mine."

I stared at him, my mouth drying out as his words sank in.

"And how do I know what you're saying is true? How do I know you're not just saying all this because you want me to love you?"

He chuckled. "I would have thought that you'd know me better than to suspect I'd mix up my own personal agenda in something as serious as this."

Remembering how quickly he'd dismissed his own sister's death, I did have trouble doubting his intentions.

The only guaranteed way I can survive this is by falling in love with Rhys. Thoughts of Kiev filled my mind. *But how? And what if I lose myself to him before I ever make it out the other end?*

Although Rhys still hadn't explained what this mysterious "process" was, I knew that I wouldn't be the same person after it. I would be like Rhys and his family. Blindly devoted to reviving the power and so-called glory of our kind. And if I wasn't like them, the process wouldn't have worked and I wouldn't have gained the powers I needed to break free from him.

It seemed like an impossible situation. In order to be strong enough to free myself, I needed to lose myself. But once I'd lost myself, would I still even want to break free?

I realized then just how desperate I was.

Even if my life ends up becoming worse, I just can't remain stagnant like this any more. Staying as I am now is guaranteed ruin. At least if I succeed at this, I'll have the ability to overcome the bonds that tie me now. I just have to pray that I'll remember what led me down this path to begin with…

"I've been trying to make it easier for you," Rhys continued, picking up a glass of blood and taking a sip. "Giving you advice on how to stay out of trouble so I don't have to punish you. I've been trying to express my own feelings for you. All to make this process easier."

I couldn't believe I was even entertaining the idea of being in love with Rhys. A few months ago, I would have been screaming at myself to stop. Now, a part of me was wishing that it was easier for me to fall for him.

"Of course," he said, "you don't *need* anybody. You could go through this all by yourself. But the chances of you losing a piece of yourself are much, much greater."

He placed his glass down on the table and looked back at the fireplace.

"What is this process?" I asked. "You still haven't told me."

He stood up and began to pace up and down the room.

"You'll know when it's time."

I looked at him in exasperation. "Can't you give me some idea?"

He breathed out impatiently.

"Whatever it is doesn't change what you have to do. You need to trust me on this."

He walked over to me and bent down so that his eyes were level with mine. His face was filled with concern.

"Mona, I don't want to risk breaking you. I've witnessed too many unsuccessful attempts to want to witness another one." I could practically see the dark memories whirling behind his eyes as he spoke.

"All right," I croaked.

Silence fell between us as we stared at each other.

Slowly, cautiously, he took a seat next to me.

"I don't know what more I can say," he breathed.

"There isn't anything more," I whispered after a pause. Bracing myself for what I was about to say, I shut my eyes. "I will love you, Rhys." I felt insane hearing myself say those words out loud.

He exhaled sharply.

I leant closer to him, brushing my cheek against his, breathing in his scent. He reached up, caressing the side of my face. I remained still. Feeling the moment, the space we were sharing.

I slipped my hand beneath his shirt, running it up along his broad, muscular chest. I shifted myself onto his lap, my legs spread out either side of him on the couch.

His expression remained serious as he held my waist.

Allowing me to take the lead. I unbuttoned his shirt and slid it off his shoulders, down his arms.

"Undress me," I whispered into his ear.

He betrayed his hunger for me as he scooped me up in his arms and laid me down in his bed. He drew out his dagger and ripped through my dress. I shivered as the tip of the blade grazed my skin. Removing the rest of his clothes, he spread himself out over me. He groaned as I pulled his face against mine and pushed my tongue between his lips. He pressed me harder into the mattress, his weight making it a struggle to breathe.

I was trying to lose myself beneath Rhys' touch. Let him envelop my heart and soul. But the harder I worked to forget the vampire, the more images of him came flooding through my brain.

No.

This is no good.

As Rhys' need began to consume him, I gripped his thick hair and tugged.

"Wait," I gasped.

He looked down at me, his eyes hooded, and frowned.

"What?"

He lifted himself up away from me and allowed me to sit up. I leaned against the headboard and buried my face in my hands.

Am I really going to risk this?

What choice do I even have now?

My throat felt parched just thinking about what I was about to do.

"Did I hurt you?" Rhys looked at me with concern.

"No, no. Rhys. I just… I think I need you to give me a memory potion."

His lips parted in surprise.

"A memory potion?"

"It's just that every time you touch me, I keep remembering the time when we were best friends," I lied. "And I find it hard to be truly intimate with you. It feels strange."

He nodded slowly.

"But not a complete memory wipe."

"No, of course not," I said quickly. I recalled one potion I had made recently before we left for The Shade. It was to test out on a human. They'd wanted to erase only select memories from his brain.

"All right," he said.

I reached out and brushed a hand over his cheek, attempting a smile.

'That way, it will be a fresh start for us."

Chapter 15: Mona

I stared at the dark green liquid. I'd concocted it in the castle's spell room with Rhys. But now that it was made, I'd asked to be left alone while I went about wiping the memories. I'd retreated to the spare bedroom of our apartment. He'd understood my desire for privacy.

I sat on the edge of the bed and reached for the jug I'd filled with the potion. I poured some into a metal goblet. Sniffing it, I almost choked from how foul it smelt.

I placed the goblet on the bedside table and stared at it. My eyes glazed over with tears and my hands were trembling.

This is it.

There will be no going back after this.

Now that I was on the verge of losing the vampire forever,

the full impact of how much I had grown to need him hit me full force. I felt winded.

What were you thinking, Mona? Of course, if you erase everything that's happened, it's unlikely that you'll ever be with him again even if you do manage by some miracle to remember to break free from Rhys. He'll be a stranger to you. And he may have already found someone else. He has no problem finding women to share his bed.

I shook my head, trying to clear my head. It was useless having these thoughts now.

Trying to steady my hand, I picked up the glass again.

I shut my eyes and took the first sip.

Before I swallowed, the memory of the first time I'd laid eyes on the vampire flashed across my mind. I forced out memory after memory with each gulp of the potion I took, each another puncture to my bleeding heart.

By the time I'd finished half of the jug, tears were streaming down my cheeks. It was hard to control my sobs.

Rhys knocked on the door. "What's wrong?" He sat down next to me on the bed.

"I'm sorry," I gasped. "It's just these memories. I'm going to miss them."

He remained silent, sitting with me for a few minutes while I cried. Then he got up and left the room again. I guessed he thought this was just something I had to work through on my own.

After I'd finished the jug, I left the room and climbed into Rhys' bed, sliding beneath the covers. He wrapped his arms around me, stroking my forehead.

As I lay there in his arms, I was determined to stay up all night. Because now those memories were alive in my mind, more vivid than ever before. And for once, I allowed myself to get lost in them. I allowed myself this one last indulgence, because by the morning, they would all be gone.

Chapter 16: Mona

When morning arrived, I woke up to feel Rhys' breathing against the nape of my neck. Whatever I'd taken that potion to forget was gone from my mind. I couldn't remember anything about it. But it must have been dear to me because my cheeks were stained with tears.

I rubbed my temples, realizing that I had a headache. And my bladder felt like it was about to burst. I'd drunk a whole jug of that liquid, after all. I rushed to the bathroom. In the mirror my skin was looking pale as usual, the circles beneath my eyes dark as ever.

When I returned to the bedroom, Rhys had woken up. He sat leaning against the headboard, looking me over as I approached the bed.

"Get dressed," he said, standing up. "I want to take you somewhere."

Once we were ready, he held my hands in his and we vanished. The next few seconds were chaos as wind howled around us. Then I felt a warm breeze against my skin and solid ground beneath my feet. Opening my eyes, I took a step back.

We were standing at the foot of a waterfall, the crash of waves filling our eardrums. I gasped at the sheer beauty of the place. The trees towered up almost higher than I could see and their leaves spread out to form a shimmering canopy, sheltering us from the sun. There were bright flowers, and butterflies the size of Rhys' hand. A lilac mist hung over the churning waters.

Then it dawned on me.

"Aviary," I gasped, looking up at Rhys.

He nodded, giving me a small smile.

Memories of being trapped here serving Arron came flooding back. I'd escaped this place. But for some reason I couldn't remember how.

"Why are we here? Isn't it dangerous?"

Rhys chuckled and shook his head.

"Not while you're with me. As to why we're here..."

He scooped me up in his arms and led me closer to the water. I thought that he was going to jump in with me. Instead, he walked around the edge of the pool and ducked behind the waterfall. The sounds were deafening now as Rhys walked into a cave behind the falling waters.

The beauty of the place took my breath away. There was a wide patch of soft moss in the center, surrounded by an array of precious stones and gems. He walked over to it and put me down. He lowered himself next to me. We both sat staring at the gushing water.

Although it felt odd, I appreciated Rhys' romantic gesture. He was making an effort to make this easier for me.

"Thank you for bringing me here," I said softly, looking up at him.

He nodded.

I reached for his hand, a few inches away from me. I held up his branded palm and ran a finger over it, tracing the outline of the black rose. I pressed my lips against the center of his palm and watched the brand come alive, even as my own rose began tingling.

Rhys raised a brow, as if asking for permission to take things further.

I lay back on the grass, never breaking eye contact with him. Slowly, he bent over me and began easing me out of my dress. Then he stood up and undressed himself. Just looking at his muscular physique made me feel weak and vulnerable.

"Kiss me," I whispered.

He leant over me and gripped both of my arms, pulling me into standing position against him. Goosebumps ran along my skin as he propped me up against the wall of the cave.

And then his lips were on mine. He kissed me slowly at first, but soon he was ravishing me. He left my lips and began pressing his mouth against my neck, sucking on my skin and grazing me with his teeth.

He touched my feet to the ground, leaving a trail of kisses as he made his way down my body. He stopped just above my navel.

I gripped his hair as he ran his hands down my legs.

"I've always loved you, Mona," he breathed against my stomach. "And I can fulfill you, if you'll just let me."

He fell silent as he began to make love to me.

It was strange. Although I'd made love to Rhys before, somehow, that morning felt like the first time.

Chapter 17: Mona

At first, I found my mind wandering occasionally, wondering what it was I had made myself forget. It was strange having a blank space in my memory. But then I stopped thinking about it. It was idiocy trying to remember. Whatever I'd forgotten, it was to help move me forward.

I was surprised by how easy it was to fall for Rhys. Over the following weeks, Rhys kept me alone with him in the castle. With his attention on me night and day, he became my life as much as I became his. It was as if nobody existed in the world but us.

His passion consumed me, so much that I couldn't help but return it. When someone desired and wanted to please you so intensely, it was hard to not reciprocate.

And that reciprocation—although small at first—set me on the right path. It was the spark that lit the fire I'd thought was long extinguished.

I found myself wanting to satisfy Rhys as he was satisfying me. I found myself wanting to bring a smile to his face, to lavish my own affections on him.

Although we remained away from everybody, he didn't just keep me on the island. He took me to some of the most beautiful places in all of the supernatural world. Most of the realms he took me to I had never visited before, some I hadn't even known existed. He romanced me in each of them.

Slowly, I found my mind becoming aligned with his. My desires beginning to match his own. I fell deeper and deeper into him.

He consumed my mind so much that I even wondered whether he was using magic on me. But I doubted it. My feelings for him had to be genuine or this whole exercise would be pointless. Rhys had told me that no magic could last during the transformation, whatever it was.

One evening, we were lying next to each other on a deserted beach in The Cove, the realm of the mermaids. I stared up at the starry night, holding his hand in mine, listening to the waves crashing against the shore. A warm breeze blew over us.

I leaned on my elbow and looked down at him. Running

a hand through his dark hair, I placed a kiss on his cheek.

"Why do you love me?" I whispered, staring into his eyes.

His Adam's apple moved as he swallowed. I thought he was about to answer, but he stood up and pulled me to my feet. Holding my hand, he led me toward the waves. He stopped once the water was at my waist.

"There's fire in you, Mona." He ran his hands through my hair. "And I don't want you to lose that."

I had no idea what he meant by fire. I thought back to my past. I couldn't remember a time since I'd left the Sanctuary that I had felt much fire in me. Except for these past few weeks with Rhys, it felt like I was gasping to keep my head above water and not be overcome by the darkness surrounding me.

"Maybe I see a piece of myself in you."

He leaned down and touched his nose against mine, closing his eyes.

We both remained silent, listening to the lapping waves around us.

I realized that whether I liked it or not, Rhys also held a piece of me now. How large a piece it was, I was beginning to be fearful of. But now that I'd let him in, I wasn't sure that I could ever fully let him out. These weeks had been so intense, just the two of us. It felt like I'd allowed him to make a mark on me that ran far deeper than my rose.

Chapter 18: Kiev

It would have been a lie to say that I didn't see it coming. I'd known what I had with Mona was temporary. Even that small respite I had bought us by kidnapping the humans had come with a heavy price.

So when she told me it was over, it was hardly a surprise. There wasn't much else either of us could do. Mona was bound to Rhys. She couldn't leave him, even if she'd wanted to be with me.

Still, I couldn't shake the frustration that had boiled up within me as she spoke the words. When she'd left the island, I'd thought it would pass, but it didn't. If anything, it grew worse.

I tried to distract myself around the island. But there

wasn't much to be distracted by other than the ghastly rituals that were held each evening. The rest of the time, there wasn't much to do. Even my siblings didn't appear busy despite the fact that we were supposed to be rulers of this island.

Helina had explained that there were often long periods of inactivity. Then suddenly, some of us would be sent on random errands that were often urgent and could take several days to complete. But most of the time they were free, as long as they turned up to the rituals in the evenings.

It was still unclear to all of us what exactly Isolde felt close to breaking through. The witches didn't discuss anything important with the vampires, confirming my suspicion that they just saw us as slaves. Pawns in whatever game they were playing. I didn't bother asking. It wasn't like there was anyone I could ask now anyway, now that Mona and Tiarni were gone. I wasn't on speaking terms with any of the other witches.

I spent as much time with my siblings as I could to take my mind off of the witch's absence. There had been such a huge gap since I last saw them that we never ran out of things to talk about. And I appreciated the time to get to know my siblings better.

I still grilled them now and then about what they'd done to Matteo. But deep down, I knew that they hadn't done it to hurt me. They had acted out of panic, thinking they were protecting me.

I felt the urge to seek out Matteo and Saira, but it was an impossible task. For one thing, my siblings told me that I was bound to this island now and wasn't allowed to leave for more than seven days without permission—thanks to their initiating me while I was drunk. I'd asked what would happen after seven days, but they refused to tell me. I wondered if they even knew themselves.

In any case, I decided that it was wise not to risk it, and Helina had made me promise that I wouldn't.

We continued to attend the rituals every night along with all the other vampires and witches on the island. It seemed that for some reason Isolde had decided to start sacrificing more than one human at a time. I assumed she thought it would make the ritual more powerful and bring her closer to whatever it was she was trying to achieve.

In any case, Isolde announced one morning at breakfast that they were running low on humans. Since Rhys was away and Efren still locked himself in the spell room all day to mourn over his sister, Isolde did something out of the ordinary.

After everybody else had left the hall, while my siblings and I had stayed back to finish our discussion, she approached us.

She cleared her throat. "I could use your help," she said.

"For what?" Erik asked.

"I think you three will be as good as any in helping me stock up on humans. I'd like you to come with me."

Erik stared from me to Helina.

"Yes," I said immediately. "We'll help."

This was perfect to take my mind off things and I'd been curious to know where they got these humans ever since I arrived on this island.

"Obviously, you are sworn to secrecy."

"Of course," Erik said, following my lead.

I was still surprised Isolde had asked us. I supposed that she knew we were all bound to this island and at their mercy, so it wasn't like there was much we could do with this knowledge. And now that her regular companions were gone, we were as good as any.

"I'm planning to leave tonight," she said. "Meet me in the courtyard after the ritual."

"Is there anything we need to bring with us?" Helina asked.

The witch stared at her. "Just your obedience."

Chapter 19: Mona

We returned to the castle early the next morning. As we arrived back in Rhys' bedroom, he closed the door and turned to face me.

"It's time for me to give you your magic back. I think you're ready."

I stared at him, my heartbeat quickening. "A-are you sure?"

He smiled and nodded.

"You've changed, Mona. I can sense when your mind is on other things, and now it's not. I am your world now."

I couldn't argue with his statement.

I sat down cross-legged in the center of the living room and he held out his palms. I closed my eyes as a flash of light hit me in the chest, and my whole body began tingling as my powers returned to me.

My knees wobbled as I stood up. I gripped the back of an armchair.

I looked at him nervously. "And now what?"

His eyes bored into mine.

"It's time to do what I've been preparing you for. We'll leave in an hour."

***

Rhys vanished us from his apartment. Once the wind stopped whirling around us, my feet hit solid ground. I opened my eyes. We were standing on a black pebble beach. A freezing wind blew against us. I drew my cloak closer.

"Where are we?" I whispered.

He didn't answer my question and instead led me toward the foot of a cliff. There was a heap of boulders at its foot. We began climbing over the boulders and soon the entrance of a cave came into view.

Rhys climbed up into the entrance and hauled me up after him. He gripped my arm, pulling me closer to him as we walked further into the cave. It was so dark now that we'd left the light of the moon, I was surprised that Rhys had a clue where he was even going. I stumbled over rocks even as he was supporting me.

"Where are we going?"

"Shh."

We walked along what felt like a winding tunnel until I could no longer see the entrance of the cave. Rhys stopped suddenly.

Metal clicked and a door opened. A stream of light flooded out. We walked through the door and found ourselves in another tunnel—but this time lanterns hung from the walls. The air felt colder now that we were traveling deeper into the mountain.

Rhys kept his grip on me. We walked forward for several minutes until we reached another old door. He gripped the rusting iron handle and with two hands twisted it open.

The temperature fell yet again. I shivered and huddled closer to Rhys. He lifted up his cloak and closed it around me as I gripped his waist.

I cast my eyes around the circular chamber we'd just entered. This chamber wasn't as well lit. There were just four large lanterns, each casting flickering shadows along the walls. The floor sloped downward toward a pool of black liquid in the center.

"What is that?"

Rhys didn't answer me as we neared it.

It was thick, yet grainy like tar. I couldn't imagine for the life of me what it was.

The liquid parted. I screamed as a woman's corpse emerged from it.

At least, I had thought it was a corpse. The woman's body shuddered as she drew in a deep rasping breath. The hall filled with a stench of decay.

Rhys clasped a hand over my mouth and pulled me a few steps back.

She reached a skeletal arm out of the water and brushed strands of black hair away from her face.

My heart hammered in my chest.

Bone protruded from the top of her forehead and her lips were shriveled. There were patches of skin missing from her nose, revealing bare cartilage. Her eyes were black as beetles, small and shrunken.

"What is she?" I breathed.

Even Rhys' breathing had quickened.

"Through us, the spirits of our Ancients live on. They still watch over us. Some more than others…"

I gasped.

"An Ancient? But I thought they were all gone long—"

"As long as we remain loyal to them, they still live and breathe with us. Lilith is the last to physically remain with us."

Lilith. It was hard to wrap my head around this thing having a name.

Rhys' eyes remained fixed on her as he spoke.

Strange words rasped from her mouth. Her voice was low and hoarse, so much that had it not been for her body, I would have assumed her to be a man.

"Only those who wish to become Channelers are admitted entrance to see her," Rhys said. "Otherwise, her existence is kept a secret."

The witch spoke in ancient witch tongue. Although Rhys had taught me to read it, I couldn't understand it when it was spoken. I looked up at Rhys, bewildered.

Rhys replied to her in the same tongue.

Then he addressed me. "She wanted to know why I've brought you here."

I stared back at the vile creature floating in the black pool. She was almost bald, except for the thin strands poking out from the front of her scalp.

Lilith spoke again. Rhys' grip around my hand tightened.

The Ancient's black eyes narrowed on me, and an eerie clucking emanated from her mouth.

I looked up at Rhys again.

"Don't break eye contact with her," he hissed, gripping my chin and forcing my head back.

I felt like I was about to throw up. The smell of the hall and her frightening eyes roaming my body made me feel violated.

She continued clucking her tongue for as long as her eyes were on me. Finally, just as it felt like I couldn't look at her anymore, she looked back at Rhys and spoke again. Her voice grated against my ears like granite.

Rhys looked back down at me.

"She… she wants to touch you."

"W-what?"

"You need to trust me," he said, glaring daggers at me.

Breathing through my mouth to avoid the stench, I inched toward the edge of the pool. My knees buckled, but as Rhys moved to help me, the witch hissed again.

Rhys stopped in his tracks.

"She wants you alone," he muttered.

The witch was watching me intently, whatever skin she had left on her lips pursed in disapproval.

I trembled as I arrived at the edge of the pond. She moved toward me.

She hissed again.

"Bend down," Rhys translated.

I bent down. Her arm shot out and gripped my hair. She tugged me closer to her. I was so close to the edge now, I almost lost my balance and fell face forward into the pool.

My whole body shivered as slimy, cold fingers brushed my forehead. I had the horrible thought that she might leave a bit of her flesh on my skin when she removed her hand.

I breathed out a sigh of relief when she finally let go of me. I scrambled back away from her, wiping my forehead with my sleeve and staring at her, panting.

Her beady eyes remained on me.

Another hiss came from her lips. Rhys' eyes had become

wide with alarm. I looked from the Ancient to Rhys, perplexed, as they went back and forth for several minutes. Finally, she bared rotten teeth and snarled at Rhys.

He fell silent and averted his eyes to the ground.

"What is she saying?" I hissed.

He looked over at me, frustration in his eyes. I managed to get to my feet and move toward him.

"Stay there." His voice boomed through the chamber.

I was taken aback by the urgency in his voice and stopped in my tracks. The witch was glaring at me. My throat felt so dry it was now painful to breathe.

Rhys spoke again to the Ancient, now sounding resigned.

The Ancient nodded slowly, her chin grazing the edge of the pool.

Then her head dipped beneath the black liquid and she vanished.

What the hell is going on?

"You can come here now," Rhys said.

I lost no time in stumbling over toward him and gripping his cloak.

"She's not convinced that you're ready." Rhys said finally.

I looked back over at the thick black liquid. The Ancient's liquid tomb was now still, as though it had never been stirred. "What?"

"She wants you to prove that you're serious first."

"Prove myself how?"

His eyes darkened.

"Doesn't she trust your judgment?" I pressed.

"She always has in the past. But with you… She wants you to do something for her first."

"What?" I was afraid to hear the answer.

Rhys paused, running a hand over his face.

"Let's get out of here first."

Chapter 20: Kiev

As planned, we met with Isolde in the courtyard a few minutes after the ritual ended. Even once she'd approached us, she still didn't offer any explanation as to our destination. She just made us all touch shoulders in a circle and we vanished from the island.

Our feet hit solid ground a few seconds later. I opened my eyes and blinked, my vision coming into focus. We were in some kind of rectangular dungeon. It appeared empty at first but on a closer look, I noticed something strange on the floor. I walked forward to see what it was.

"Wait," Isolde scolded, gripping my arm and pulling me back. "Follow after me."

She walked forward and we followed.

As I approached within five feet of it, realization hit me like a brick.

A dark hole in the floor extended downward to form a tunnel. Its walls were made of a swirling, translucent substance. And beyond the walls lay a sea of endless black scattered with stars.

My siblings' faces looked how I felt inside. They had seen one of these too. When they were first brought to Cruor from the Blood Keep.

This was a gate to the human realm.

I wondered now how many more gates remained secretly open and where they were. It brought back unwanted memories of the redhead girl I'd fallen for. Sofia. I'd said goodbye to her standing outside a gate like this. She'd given me one last glance before she let go of the edge and hurtled down into the abyss. The gate had closed soon afterward.

Prying my eyes away from the hole and swallowing hard, I looked again around the dungeon again.

"Where are we?"

"That's not important," Isolde said curtly. "Now, I'm sure you all know what this is."

We nodded.

"So I'll jump first, and you follow a few seconds after me, one at a time. All right?"

"All right," Helina said, although she was trembling. I supposed her last memories on earth had been so traumatic that she now associated the human realm with pain.

I wrapped an arm round her shoulder. There wasn't much I could say to comfort her though when I myself had not the slightest clue where we'd end up.

Isolde jumped through and disappeared.

"You go next, Erik," I said.

He cleared his throat and nodded, stepping forward. He glanced up at us before diving in after her.

"And now you, Helina," I said.

She trembled as she neared the edge of the gate. The suction began pulling at her hair. She jumped through.

And then it was my turn.

I was sucked down through that tunnel so fast I couldn't keep my eyes open. The air pressure squeezed my body, making it hard to even gasp for air.

I landed on a hard surface. I climbed to my feet and looked around. We were in another dimly lit dungeon. Had I been a human I would have been shivering already. The cold was biting, the type that gnawed at your bones.

"Good," Isolde said, straightening out her long black gown. "Follow me."

She grabbed a chain of keys from a hook on the wall. She walked toward a wooden door in the corner of the chamber and pushed it open. We followed her up a set of narrow stone steps. We emerged through a trapdoor into a hall. Black chandeliers hung from the high ceiling. There was a click as Isolde locked the trapdoor behind us.

We crossed the room and passed through a door that led to a circular hall. There was a door to our right, and a staircase in the center leading upward. Architecturally, this place was similar in design to the castle back in my siblings' island, and also Rhys' island. Even the long drapes were made of similar fabric.

I looked out of the stained-glass window nearest me. I was shocked firstly to see how high up we were. This building—or castle, it seemed—was built on the peak of a high mountain. There was thick snow everywhere. In the distance at the foot of the mountain was a forest, as evidenced by the white treetops, and further still in the distance was the sea.

Where on earth are we?

"Annora," Isolde called, her voice echoing off the walls.

I turned around. A tall young woman with long black hair and cold grey eyes descended the wide staircase. She wore a long black dress which trailed on the ground, similar to Isolde. Evidently also a witch.

I left the window and rejoined my siblings, who were watching Isolde talking to this stranger.

"We've come for more," Isolde said, rubbing her palms together.

"Well, you know where to find them," Annora replied, her voice smooth like silk. "Take what you need. We're due for another batch soon."

Her eyes glanced over me and my siblings briefly and she raised a brow.

"New recruits, I see. No Rhys and Efren this time?"

Isolde shook her head.

"It's complicated," Isolde said. She paused and looked at my siblings and I. She held out her ring of keys and Erik took them from her. She pointed toward a door in the far corner of the room. "That's the kitchen. In the far right corner, you'll find the entrance to another dungeon. You have the keys—it's the large bronze one, and the smaller bronze ones will unlock the cells. Go in and bring out a dozen or so humans. Herd them out here. Don't let any of them scramble away. We don't have time to go chasing after them. And only take humans from the first four cells. Do not go further than that. Understood?"

"Yes, Isolde," Helina replied.

Isolde turned back to continue her conversation with Annora.

We swept toward the kitchen. Erik found the entrance to the dungeon and we descended the steps.

It was dark inside. The smell of fresh, hot human blood was intoxicating. I began to salivate. Screams and cries echoed around the dungeon as soon as they realized we had entered.

Erik unlocked the door of the first cell, which contained half a dozen humans, and, with the help of Helina, started grabbing humans and pulling them out.

I was about to help them when I smelt it. A type of blood that was a rarity to our kind. Its sweetness was intoxicatingly familiar. And it reminded me of Sofia. This was the blood of an immune—a rare species of human who couldn't be turned into a vampire.

Unable to resist following the scent, I rushed past the first four cells.

"Kiev!" Erik hissed. "What are you doing? She said—"

"I know what she said," I snapped. "Just keep quiet. I'll join you in a minute."

I ventured deeper into the dungeon until it was beginning to appear less populated. I looked around, but the scent kept leading me further and further until eventually the cells I walked by had nobody in them… except for one.

I stopped short. I peered through the cell and saw a dark figure huddled in the corner.

I placed my hands against the bars and looked closer. It was a woman. She was sitting with her head resting against her bunched-up knees. She appeared to be… pregnant.

She looked up and gasped. She huddled closer into the corner, staring at me with fear. I took a step back. The color of her eyes had sent shivers down my spine. They were bright green. For one uncanny moment, it felt like I was looking at Sofia who had once been my own pregnant captive.

This woman's hair was black though, and now that I

could see her face, she appeared to be well in her thirties. But although she wasn't Sofia, there was something about her that made me believe that I'd seen her face before somewhere. Green eyes, black hair. Soft, gentle features.

Think, Kiev. Think.

"Brother!" Helina called anxiously.

"I'm coming," I yelled.

I stared at her once more. And then it hit me.

Anna. She was Sofia's friend, and the only other immune who'd inhabited the Novaks' island. She'd been there in Aviary too, just as I'd let Sofia go.

But how can it be? How could she have aged so quickly? I haven't been gone long from Earth.

I remembered her as a young woman in her late teens or early twenties. Now, though still beautiful, she appeared to be at least thirty.

"I've seen you before," I whispered. "Anna?"

"Kiev," she breathed, her eyes widening. I was surprised she recognized me, since my eyes hadn't yet returned to red since Mona's disappearance. They were still green, like hers.

"What are you doing here?" I asked, eyeing her protruding stomach.

"Kiev!" Erik bellowed.

"Shut up!" I hissed. "I said I'm coming."

I turned back to Anna, now looking at her with urgency.

"I-I was kidnapped here," she said, her voice cracking. "I

don't know what they want with me."

She looked terribly thin for a woman as pregnant as her and she had dark shadows under her eyes, her skin pale. They weren't feeding her enough. I didn't need to be a physician to know that she might not make it until birth if she remained here.

I didn't know why, but panic coursed through my veins. I sped back over to my siblings and snatched the keys from Helina's hands. Ignoring my siblings' protests, I raced back toward Anna.

It was as though my intelligence had shut down and I was acting on sheer adrenaline, all consequences forgotten.

I unlocked her cell and ripped open the gate. She screamed as I towered over her. I crouched down and placed a hand over her mouth.

"I'm not going to hurt you," I whispered into her ear. "I know you've every reason not to trust me after everything you know about me. But I swear, I'll not hurt you. You need to get out of here. If only for your baby's sake, come with me. This is a risk you have to take."

Her breathing became slower and she stopped fighting against me. Though her eyes were still filled with distrust and fear, desperation took over.

"Just don't say a word and keep close to me."

I ripped off my cloak and swung it over her shoulders, attempting to cover her large stomach as much as possible. I pulled the hood over her head to cast a shadow over her face.

Scooping her up in my arms, I arrived back just a few seconds before Isolde came walking down the steps, giving me time to place her feet down on the ground next to the other humans.

"You're ready?" she asked, casting her eyes around the group of humans.

I gripped Anna's shoulder, keeping her positioned close to me and shielding her as much as possible from Isolde's view by guiding her to walk behind the other humans. It was a blessing that my siblings had picked out some tall men from the cells. My cloak did something to hide her bulging form, but it wasn't enough for me to feel confident allowing her to walk in clear view of the witch.

Erik and Helina eyed me and Anna nervously but didn't say anything now that Isolde was present. We herded the humans out of the prison and made our way through the castle back to the dungeon where the gate was. We gathered them all close to the hole in the floor and Isolde began pushing humans through one at a time. I kept a tight grip on Anna's arm. As Isolde turned on the last few humans, I stepped forward.

"I may as well do the rest," I said.

Her eyes rested on me questioningly. Then she grunted and jumped through the gate. I pushed the rest of the humans through except for Anna.

I looked at my siblings.

"You two go next."

They stared at me and Anna again.

"Kiev, what is going—"

Before she could finish her question, I pushed her into the gate. Erik understood that now was not the time to ask questions and he jumped in after Helina.

Then I looked down at Anna. Her face had drained of all blood as she looked down at the abyss. She gripped her stomach.

"I don't know if I can—"

"You've no choice. You either come with me… or you get locked up again in that prison."

I held my hand out to her. She bit her lip and, trembling, reached for my hand.

"I suggest I go down with you at the same time. I might be able to cushion you somewhat on the other side."

I fastened the cloak tighter around her, and moved her toward the edge of the tunnel. I stood behind her, her back as close to my chest as possible. I felt her shiver against me as I wrapped my arms around her waist. And then I pushed us both in.

As we fell, I did my best to keep her close to me, and on the other end, I just about managed to protect her from the fall by pulling her on top of me as we landed on the stone floor. Still, she looked like she was about to throw up and she clutched her stomach, gasping in pain.

I scrambled to my feet to block Isolde's view of her and helped her to her feet.

Fortunately, the group of humans was standing in front of us so Isolde hadn't seen me come through with Anna. I made sure the cloak was covering her properly and looked over the crowd to see Isolde was already forming all the humans into a circle with the help of my siblings.

I assisted them, making sure that Anna was next to me. Once everyone had formed a circle and were all touching each other, we vanished.

Chapter 21: Mona

I was gasping for air by the time we reached the entrance of the cave. I breathed in deeply. Each second that Rhys delayed telling me what the witch had said was another second the knot in my stomach tightened.

"Tell me now, Rhys." I gripped his shirt.

"She... she wants to test out your mind first. How strong, how obedient it is."

I stared at him.

"So let me get this straight. The transformation in itself is a huge ordeal that most people don't survive. Yet she wants me to do something else in addition?"

He nodded. He held my hand and started helping me down the boulders back toward the pebbly beach.

"What more does she want from me?"

"I don't know."

"What? How can you not know? I just saw her talking to—"

"She wouldn't tell me exactly what it was she wanted. She just said that she wanted you in that chamber for a few hours… without me."

I stared at him, barely believing my ears.

"But… all along the plan was for you to guide me through, be my rock—"

He gripped my shoulders and shook me.

"Yes," he said, glaring down at me. "That still is the plan. I'll be by your side. But she wants you alone with her beforehand."

"Why wouldn't she tell you what she was going to do with me?" I croaked.

"I don't know. I tried to pry for an answer but she refused to give me details."

"Alone, in there, for hours." I repeated the words slowly, letting them sink in, images of that nightmarish chamber flooding my mind.

"You have an hour to decide. If we don't return in an hour, she'll assume you're not serious."

I bit my lip as it trembled.

Although the prospect made me want to forget gaining Rhys' powers and just return to my old life, I knew that I couldn't. I'd come this far. And now this was the final step. I just couldn't give up now.

"I'll do it," I murmured.

Concern filled Rhys' eyes as he held my hands against his chest.

We both remained silent as we looked at each other. Perhaps he was studying me to see if this really was what I wanted.

Then he nodded.

"Very well. If you're sure. I'll be keeping track of the time and I'll return to the chamber as soon as the period is over."

He walked with me back up to the entrance of the cave and through the first dark tunnel. Once we reached the first corridor that was lit, he let go of me and took a step back into the shadows.

"You need to walk alone from here," he said.

"All right," I whispered.

I glanced once more at Rhys, hoping to draw some sort of strength from him before I left him.

"Wait." He removed his belt and fastened it around my waist along with the silver dagger that was attached to it. He pressed my palm against the hilt. "You might need this for whatever Lilith has planned."

I gulped and looked down the shadowy hallway. As I turned to leave, he caught my arm and pulled me flush against him, kissing me hard.

When he drew away, his eyes were blazing.

"You're strong enough to get through this." He spoke the words aggressively. "Do you trust me?"

I stared at him, my lips still tingling from the force of his kiss.

"Yes," I said. And for perhaps the first time in my life, I truly meant it.

Chapter 22: Kiev

We all reappeared outside the castle in the courtyard where we'd first vanished with Isolde.

We herded the humans up the castle steps and into the entrance hall. Then Isolde turned to me, since I was closest to her, and handed me another set of keys.

"Take them down to the dungeon and make sure the cells are shut properly. We don't want any more escapes."

I nodded and took the keys. She went in the opposite direction and my siblings and I led the humans toward the dungeon. I opened up the trapdoor and we bundled them inside. Anna was the last. I picked her up and walked down with her. I called up the trapdoor to my siblings, "I'll take things from here. You two can go."

When they looked hesitant to leave me alone I shot them both glares and they did as I'd suggested.

As soon as they had disappeared from sight, I picked up Anna again and, locking the trapdoor behind me, made a dash across the entrance hall up the stairs.

"Where are you taking me?" she gasped, clutching my neck.

"Shh."

I was worried I'd bump into someone in the corridors or the staircases so I moved as fast as I could. I heaved a sigh of relief as we reached my apartment. I swung the door open and slammed it shut behind me. I walked into my bedroom, placing Anna down on the soft bed.

I ran around the apartment making sure all the windows and balcony doors were closed.

I returned to the bedroom to see Anna huddle up into the corner of the bed, breathing heavily as she clutched her stomach.

"Why are you doing this?" she croaked.

I stopped still and stared at her.

Why am I doing this?

I wasn't sure that I knew myself.

I ignored her question and asked one of my own.

"How old are you?" I couldn't contain my curiosity any longer.

"I-I'll be thirty-five soon."

Thirty-five.

"How old were you when I last saw you?"

"I was eighteen."

I swore.

Seventeen years.

"How is that possible?"

She swallowed hard before replying, her voice still trembling. "I think time passes differently when you're here in this realm... with these witches."

"How do you know?"

"I overheard a couple of vampires talking, back in the dungeon. Time passes slower compared to on Earth."

I rubbed my head, trying to let this insane truth sink in. Several minutes passed in silence.

"The Shade," I muttered. "That still exists and... the Novaks still rule it?"

She nodded.

The Novaks. My own distant family. Another insanity I was still trying to wrap my head around.

Noticing she was shivering, I snapped back to the reality I now faced. The challenges I had to overcome. I untucked the blanket from the bed and handed it to her. She wrapped it around her, still staring at me suspiciously.

"Stay here," I said. "I'll be back in a few minutes. I warn you—do not leave this room."

I flew out the door and rushed down the staircases toward

the kitchen.

I knew that we had proper food in this castle because I'd seen witches eat it. They drank blood but they also ate regular food.

I hunted around the kitchen and found soup in one of the big cooking pots. There was bread on the counter too. I found a tray and, heating up the soup quickly, poured a portion into a bowl. I grabbed the whole loaf of bread, a water jug and a metal goblet, placing everything on the tray.

I covered the tray with a towel I found hanging on a hook and hoped I wouldn't bump into anyone on my way back up. I rushed back up to my room and slammed the door shut behind me. Anna hadn't moved from where I'd left her.

I placed the meal on the bed next to her and removed the towel.

"Eat," I muttered.

She looked at the food doubtfully, but she soon gave into her hunger. She swallowed down the soup and finished the whole loaf of bread in less than ten minutes. Then she drank half the jug of water.

While she was eating, I lit up the fireplace, warming the cold room.

When she was done, she leaned back on the bed. Some warmth had already returned to her cheeks.

Now that she had some food in her, my next concern was the smell of her blood. This castle was filled with vampires and her scent was a siren call to my kind. I'd closed all the windows and doors and drawn all the curtains. But I feared that some might have already detected her scent. I feared it was so strong they might be able to smell it through the walls.

I looked back at her.

"Take a shower," I said.

She raised her eyebrows at me but she didn't protest. I guessed that she was grateful for the opportunity to clean herself.

I placed a clean towel and a fresh set of my own night clothes in the bathroom. They'd be too large for her but she'd have to make do with them.

While she was in the bathroom, I sat down on the bed.

What am I going to do?

The scent of her blood was getting to my head, making it hard to concentrate. I fought back the urge to dig my fangs into her soft neck.

Hell, never mind hiding her from the others, I'm going to need to hide her from myself if I don't get a hold on myself.

I forced my mind back to the matter at hand. *How do I mask the scent of her blood?*

I racked my brains, trying to recall any smell that was stronger than immune blood.

I knew there were ways to dilute the scent—like placing jugs of regular human blood in my room. Still, it wasn't foolproof and having lots of human blood in my room in addition to her sweet smell could just attract more attention.

One of Mona's charms really would be useful right now...

I realized that for now, the best thing I could do was steal some of Helina's perfume and have Anna coat herself with it. I'd have to leave the room as little as possible, and not allow anyone in.

"What happened to you, Kiev?" Anna's soft voice broke through my thoughts.

She was standing leaning against the bathroom door, wearing my pajamas.

"What?" I frowned at her.

"Well... your eyes, for one thing."

"Don't get too used to them. They flicker back and forth."

She walked over to the bed and sat down on the edge of it, stretching out her legs.

"I don't know what this place is, why you rescued me from that dungeon or what you intend to do with me but... I don't know. You just seem different to the man I knew in Aviary, who stole a newborn from his helpless mother."

Her green eyes were full of honesty.

I cleared my throat and stood up, suddenly uncomfortable beneath her gaze.

"Whose child are you bearing?"

"Kyle's, my husband's."

Kyle. The name rang a bell. He was one of the last vampires I'd seen back in Aviary. He'd been taken there along with Anna and another human boy. He was there the night I let them all escape.

Silence fell between us for several minutes.

"I don't know why I saved you," I said. "And I also don't know what I'm going to end up doing with you. So don't get too comfortable around me."

I walked closer to her. She flinched as I reached out to touch her forehead.

Her temperature seemed normal. "If you lie down flat, I'll check on your baby," I said.

She looked at me doubtfully, but took me up on my suggestion. She lay down on the bed and lifted the shirt up to reveal her stomach.

She shivered as I placed my cold hands over her bump. I ran my hands over her skin, feeling her stomach at various points. Then I spread out both of my palms flat. Finally, I placed my ear against her stomach.

Sensing a healthy amount of movement, I pulled the shirt back over her. I stood up and she sat back up in bed, still staring at me.

"I need to get back to Earth," she said. "My family and everyone at The Shade will be worried sick about me. I don't know how much time is passing there each second that I'm here, but I'm scared it will be too long and they will lose all hope. I have two other children, Kiev."

Her eyes were now brimming with tears.

I heaved a sigh.

I knew that she had to get back, but I had no idea how that would ever happen. Right now the best thing I could do was concentrate on protecting her and her unborn child from others, and from myself.

Chapter 23: Mona

Each step I took toward the circular chamber panicked my mind further. I tried to focus on Rhys' last assurance to me before I left him.

I paused just outside the door.

I don't even understand a word she says. How am I going to do this?

I pushed the door and it creaked open. I peeked my head inside and shut the door behind me. I inched over to the edge of the raised floor and looked down at the pool. The witch hadn't surfaced. Although the stench had dissipated somewhat, it would return full force as soon as she appeared again.

My knees about to give way again, I walked down toward

the pool.

I cleared my throat.

"I'm back," I said, my voice cracking.

My voice echoed around the walls.

I waited with bated breath. But the witch didn't resurface.

Perhaps she didn't hear me?

I lowered myself to my knees and leant over the liquid, speaking louder. "Uh, excuse me. Lilith? I'm back. I've decided to—"

A powerful gust blew from behind me. I could barely scream before I fell face forward into the dark liquid.

In my shock, I opened my mouth to gasp for air, only to choke on a lungful of black liquid. I kicked and moved my arms frantically, trying to surface. I had underestimated how thick the liquid was. Each movement I made was ten times harder than it should have been.

I gripped the side of the pool, hauling myself up and retching. The pool's rotten taste overwhelmed my senses. I clambered to pull myself out, but something closed around my ankle. I was yanked back down into the liquid with such force I lost my grip on the edge of the pool and was submerged once more.

I was pulled down further and further into the grave of this rotting corpse.

I did my best to keep my mouth shut this time, but my oxygen was running out fast. In my panic, I couldn't think of any charm that could help me to breathe.

The grasp around my ankle didn't loosen for a second. It only got tighter the further I was pulled. It felt like my hip might dislocate from the force.

My lungs were now screaming with pain. They felt like they were about to burst. As I felt I was seconds away from dying, my head bobbed above the black liquid. I opened my mouth and gasped for air. Wiping the fluid from my eyes, I opened them only to be met with pitch darkness.

I spread out my hands and felt stone walls all around me. When I reached my hand upward, it brushed a low rough ceiling. I was trapped in some sort of narrow container.

I was terrified that the hand would once again clasp around my ankle and pull me back into the black substance. I tried to push on the ceiling, but it didn't budge.

Where am I?

No sooner had I asked myself the question than there was a loud crack. I looked up to see the ceiling had popped open. Except that this was no ceiling. It was a lid.

I reached up to push the lid again and this time it was much easier to budge. Careful not to submerge myself, I pushed at it until it slid off. I reached up and gripped hold of the ledge. I kicked and managed to heave myself over after several attempts. I found myself rolling onto a patch of grass. I coughed, remains of that foul substance still coating my mouth.

I sat up and gasped to see that I'd just climbed out of a grave. And now that I looked around, I was surrounded by marble tombstones.

It took a few seconds to realize where I was.

The Sanctuary.

My old home.

I remembered playing hide and seek in this graveyard with Rhys as a child.

I looked around in awe. I'd lost track of how much time had passed since I'd set foot in The Sanctuary. But my awe soon turned to panic. I'd been banished. I couldn't be seen here. It wasn't even possible to enter the boundaries of The Sanctuary without permission. Clearly this Ancient was able to bypass their protective spell.

I turned back around to look at the grave I'd just climbed out of. I almost screamed as I caught sight of the Ancient's beady black eyes glaring up at me, her irises glinting in the moonlight.

She began talking to me, her voice hoarse and grating.

I held up my hands. "I don't understand you," I whispered. I shook my head forcefully. "I can read your language but I can't understand."

She scowled and, lifting two bony hands onto the grass, pulled herself out of the grave. I took a step back as she stood up, revealing her full height for the first time.

I gasped at how tall she was. Almost twice my height.

Black cloth covered her body—I assumed it had once been a dress, but it was so ripped and ragged that it now showed more of her body than it concealed.

I stared in horror as she staggered over to one of the other gravestones, her sickeningly thin legs shaking as if they could barely carry her own weight. She bent down, her back folding sharply, and picked up a stone from the grass. She walked over to a slab of black stone and began scratching against it. She dropped the stone and stood up.

I waited for her to step back before approaching the stone. It was hard to concentrate on the text with her rasping breathing behind me. The more I read, the more I wanted to look away. The more I wished that I had never started reading.

My body was shaking more than ever as I drew my eyes away from it and crumpled to the grass. The Ancient's eyes narrowed on me, as though she were studying my reaction.

I stared at her in disbelief.

She began clucking her tongue impatiently.

I managed to get to my feet and walked over to the slab. Picking up the stone, I wrote my agreement in her language.

She hissed at me and gestured toward the exit of the graveyard. A pair of tall gates.

I didn't need her to show me the way. I'd been here a thousand times in my youth. I watched as she crawled back into the grave and lowered herself, disappearing from sight as she replaced the stone lid over her.

I looked up at the old clock tower outside the entrance of the graveyard. I didn't have much time. The Ancient had given a strict deadline.

The first thing I did was clean myself of the liquid using my magic. Then, putting an invisibility spell over myself, I weaved through the tombstones until I reached the gates. I looked around the street outside. It appeared to be empty.

As I walked, it felt like I was walking to my death. There were witches here still far more powerful than I was. Killing fellow witches wasn't allowed, but I was an outcast. I knew that they wouldn't hesitate to end me if given the chance.

I guessed this was part of my test. How much was I willing to put on the line?

As I walked through the city, a wave of déjà vu crashed over me. Hardly anything about this peaceful place had changed since I'd left. The white architecture, domes studded with gems; the blue lakes and fresh pastures; the waterfall crashing in the distance; the breeze kissing my skin… my home. My heart ached for what I'd lost. This realm wasn't called The Sanctuary for no reason. It was everything that the abode of the Ancients' witches was not.

I imagined these streets during the daytime. A few days after my parents had died, I'd been dragged down this very road, blood pouring from my nose after the beating I'd received, to be thrown off of the island. I breathed in deeply, trying to control the emotions coursing through me.

I deliberately took a turning to avoid the street where I had grown up. I wasn't sure I could handle that without breaking down and sobbing.

My mother, father, all my siblings, aunts, uncles… I was responsible for all of their deaths. Rhys was the closest thing I had to family now.

I was thankful at least that the Ancient was making me do this at night, rather than in the daytime when the streets would be teeming with witches. As it was, I already had to dodge a few couples who were out taking a stroll.

I walked through the residential area until I reached the foot of a hill. At the top of it was the abode of the ruler of The Sanctuary. The Ageless.

My breath hitched as I looked up at the white marble palace. As I climbed up the steps, my heart raced. My conscience screamed at me to stop and turn around. But I was too far gone for that now.

I reached the top of the hill and walked around the palace, studded with rubies that glinted beneath the moonlight.

I scanned the second floor until I spotted a balcony. I transported myself up there, and was relieved to see a balcony door had been left open, to let in the warm breeze no doubt.

I tried to quieten my breathing as I stepped into a circular bedroom. In the center was a gold-framed bed, where a beautiful woman with long silver hair lay asleep in the arms of a man, both bare except for the silk sheet covering them. I walked over to the end of their bed and cast a charm on them that would impair their hearing while I was searching for what the Ancient had sent me for.

I cast my eyes around the chamber. On spotting a row of cabinets in the corner, I began rummaging through them as fast as I could. I moved from room to room and by the eighth one, I was beginning to lose hope I'd ever find it in time.

But then I saw it, as I was rummaging through a small cupboard at the bottom of the staircase. Wrapped up in dark blood orange leather was a heap of maps, printed on old yellowing parchment. I curled up the leather binding and tucked it securely beneath my cloak.

Now for part two.

I climbed back up the staircase, approaching the Ageless' bedroom cautiously. She and her lover were still asleep. I felt the hilt of the silver dagger in my belt. I withdrew it as I approached the bed.

Gripping the Ageless' hair, I sliced through her neck.

She wasn't even able to scream before her windpipe was severed. Blood stained the white sheets. The man woke up, but before he could move, I'd cut his throat too.

And then I ran.

I rushed to the balcony and jumped off. I sped down the

hill and ran as fast as my legs could carry me, back to the graveyard.

Weaving between the tombstones, I arrived back at the stone where I was due to meet the Ancient. I looked up at the clock tower. I was early. I crouched down and tried to start moving the lid. It budged slightly and eventually I managed to pull it off. I decided that it was better to wait in hiding beneath the tombstone than out in the open after what I'd just done.

I lowered myself back into the liquid. And soon enough, a clammy hand reached out and gripped my ankle, pulling me back down into the darkness where I belonged.

Chapter 24: Kiev

I left Anna locked in the bathroom when I climbed up to Helina's floor. I stopped outside her door and placed my ear against it. I didn't detect any sounds coming from inside so I turned the door knob—unlocked as usual. Nobody in this castle seemed to be concerned about locking doors except me.

I crept along the hallway and headed straight for my sister's bedroom. I glanced over at her dressing table, scanning it for some kind of perfume. There were several bottles. I grabbed the nearest one.

Then I raced back to the entrance. My stomach rose into my throat as I opened the front door to see Helina standing outside, about to push the door open.

Her eyes widened.

"Kiev. What are you doing?"

"I was looking for you," I bluffed, slipping the bottle beneath my cloak.

"What for?"

"I wanted to check if rituals are resuming as usual tonight."

"Yes, why wouldn't they?"

"All right. That was all." I turned and sped off in the opposite direction.

"Wait, I need to talk to you too," she called after me, but I ignored her.

My heart hammering in my chest, I raced back toward my room and locked myself inside. I knocked on the bathroom door.

"Anna," I whispered through the door. "I'm back."

No answer.

"Anna?"

I knocked.

I heard a retching sound and then a weak voice. "Yeah… I'm here."

"Open the door."

The door opened slowly and Anna appeared, her face pale as she wiped vomit away from her mouth with a tissue.

"What's wrong?"

"I don't know. I'm wondering if it's something to do with

the meal you gave me. Either you poisoned it, or my stomach has forgotten how to digest proper food."

I stared at her. I doubted that there was anything wrong with the food I'd given her. It had smelled fresh enough.

She finished wiping herself down and got back into bed, shivering as she pulled the covers back over her.

I handed her the bottle of perfume.

"You need to cover yourself with this. Use the whole bottle if you have to."

"Puke and perfume," she muttered, eyeing the small bottle. "Great."

She sighed and got out of bed again, walking toward the bathroom with the bottle and closing the door. I waited outside the door until she'd finished.

She stepped out after several minutes, holding up the empty bottle. "Ugh, I reek."

The scent of her blood was still very noticeable to me, but the perfume masked it a lot better than I had thought it would. It was strong stuff.

She began walking back over to the bed, but her knees gave way before she reached it.

I caught her just before she made contact with the floor.

"I feel d-dizzy," she gasped, her eyes shut tight.

I carried her over to the bed and laid her down on it, pulling the covers over her. Worry gripped me as I looked at her fragile state. "I'm going to need to find some more food for you. You can try to eat it again in a few hours. You have to get something in you."

She looked up at me weakly and nodded. "I'll try."

I felt her forehead. It felt warmer than before. Too warm. I placed two fingers against her neck. Her pulse felt weak. Something wasn't right.

There was a knock at the door.

Anna looked up at me, panic filling her eyes. I scooped her up and rushed her back into the bathroom.

"Lock the door," I hissed.

When the bathroom door bolted shut, I answered the front door. I breathed out in relief to see that it was just my brother.

"Erik? What do you want?"

He was about to open his mouth, but he paused as he sniffed the air.

My stomach churned.

"That smell… women's perfume?"

"Oh, Helina. She visited me." I cringed internally, praying that he wouldn't confirm this with our sister.

"Helina, huh?"

His eyes darkened, his face shrouded. His chest began to heave and then, to my shock, he gripped my shirt and shook me.

"You've been sleeping with Julisse!" he hissed.

Julisse?

I gripped my brother's hands and yanked them away, his claws tearing through my shirt in the process.

"What the hell are you talking about?"

"That's Julisse's perfume."

"No! This is Helina's perfume."

"Don't lie to me, Kiev."

He launched at me with speed I'd forgotten my brother possessed. I staggered back and attempted to slam the door against his face, but it was too late. He'd entered the apartment and was beginning to rip my bedroom apart. Upending tables and tearing through curtains.

I was stunned. I couldn't remember ever witnessing my brother lose his temper like this.

I leapt on him and wrestled him to the ground. I held him in a choke until his breathing became a little steadier.

"You dare accuse me of sleeping with my own brother's woman?"

He scoffed. "You sleep with enough women to lose track of who belongs to whom."

"I've never touched Julisse," I growled, tightening my grip around him.

"Then explain why your room reeks of her perfume," he choked.

I breathed out in frustration. *Helina must have been borrowing the bottle from Julisse.*

"I took the perfume from Helina's room."

"Oh, to satisfy your lifelong urge to try out women's perfume?"

I knocked his head against the wooden floor.

I held my breath. I knew now that he wouldn't believe any other explanation but the truth. But the memory of the way he'd stormed Matteo's island was still too fresh. I didn't trust him, just as he didn't trust me.

"I'm telling you, I'm not sleeping with your woman," I said through gritted teeth. "I don't need to explain my every movement to you, and if you don't believe me, you can go to—"

A retching came from the bathroom.

I swore.

That second of distraction became my downfall. Erik kneed me in the stomach, loosening my hold around him. He scrambled toward the bathroom and forced the door open with one powerful kick.

His mouth fell open as he stared at the floor.

"No," I hissed, rushing to block his view of Anna.

But it was too late.

She was crouched over the toilet, vomiting again. Her whole body trembled.

Erik took a step back, dumbstruck.

"I-I'm sorry," he stammered.

"You'll be more than sorry once I'm through with you," I growled.

I saw red and lunged at him, flooring him once again. I dealt him one blow after the other until his face was a bloody mess.

"Stop!"

I glanced up to see Helina entering the room, her hands clasped over her mouth. She hurried over and hauled me away from Erik.

Erik staggered to his feet and crumpled to the floor in a corner of the room, breathing heavily.

"What the hell is going on in here?" Helina demanded. She paused, sniffing the air. "And why does this room smell of Julisse's perfume?" She narrowed her eyes on me and gripped my collar. "Have you been the one sleeping with Erik's girl?"

"Stop, Helina," Erik muttered.

I breathed out in frustration, brushing her away. There was no point trying to hide it any more. Erik knew and of course he would tell his sister.

I walked over to the bathroom and pointed to Anna crouched down on the floor.

Helina gasped. "This human… you stole her from the back of that dungeon." Tears of fear and panic welled in her eyes. "No. No, Kiev. I don't like this. I don't like this at all. Please. We need to return her. If we do it now, Isolde might still—"

"No," I growled, pushing her back.

"There are so many other girls on this island, why do you have to—"

"Shut your mouth and listen for once," I snarled. I towered over her, glaring from her to my brother. "What's going to happen now is very simple. You two are going to leave this room and pretend you never saw her."

"But Kiev—"

"If either of you so much as breathe a word about this human or harm her in any way, I swear—it's over. I'll find a way to leave this island and you'll never see me again."

That shut my sister up. She chewed on her lower lip.

"I've been lenient enough to still talk to you after what you did to Matteo. But this is your last chance. You need to stop trying to judge what's best for me and just do what I tell you to do. Now, you're either with me or against me."

There was a silence, interrupted only by more retching from Anna. It irritated me that I was wasting all this time trying to keep my siblings in check when Anna was in need of me.

"You do realize what will happen if we get caught?" Erik said. His face had almost healed by now.

I grunted. I didn't know what punishment we would face. But it wouldn't make a difference.

Helina sank down on the bed. Her eyes glazed over as she stared at the wall.

"So are you with me, or against me?"

I glared down at both of my siblings.

"Of course we're not against you," Erik said.

Helina nodded, gulping.

"We're not against you," she repeated.

"But are you with me?"

They both nodded.

Truth be told, a part of me had expected them to refuse.

"And I'm sorry, Kiev," Erik said, still sitting on the floor, now holding his head in his hands. "Julisse has been a sore spot for me recently."

I stared at Erik. "What do you mean?"

He heaved a sigh, rubbing a palm against his forehead. "She's started cheating on me. I know it. But I can't prove it. And, of course, she won't admit to it."

I was at a loss for what to say. I'd never had had much conviction about their relationship—Julisse had a way about her that made me distrust her. But I was surprised that she would cheat on my brother. He was certainly one of the best-looking men on the island and also appeared to be several years younger than her.

But with Anna half dying on my bathroom floor, now was not the time for me to be a relationship counsellor to my brother.

"Well, I'm sorry to hear that," I said curtly.

Erik got up and walked toward me. He held out his hand and shook mine, patting me on the shoulder.

"I'm sorry for accusing you. I guess I didn't believe you would do something like that to me. I was just venting."

I nodded.

Helina stood up and gripped my arm.

"I'm sorry too," she said softly. "And now, I promise, we're on your side. I don't know why you want this pregnant woman so much, or what you plan to do with her—to be honest, I'd rather not know. But whatever insane plan you have going through your mind, we'll not say a word."

She would have been even more horrified to learn that I had not even an insane plan. I had no plan at all.

They headed for the front door and stepped out into the corridor outside.

"Wait," I hissed, just before they left. "Helina. Bring me down the rest of your perfume, will you?"

Chapter 25: Mona

I'd thought that I would feel more shaken after murdering the ruler of The Sanctuary and her lover in their sleep. But I just felt numb. Perhaps it was Rhys' influence on me finally working. I'd done what I had to do. Now that I'd done it, it felt almost no different than any other mundane task he might ask me to do.

When I resurfaced, I was back in Lilith's cave. Gasping, I climbed out of the pool and pulled out the rolls of parchment beneath my cloak. They were soaked. Before they could disintegrate, I dried them with my magic, thankful to see that they were still readable. I turned back to face the Ancient, who was now floating in the pool. I held out the leather binder to her.

She crawled out of the pool and towered over me, snatching it from me. She flipped through the pages with her bony fingers. Seemingly satisfied, she handed it back to me. I was confused. I didn't know what I was supposed to do with them. Hell, I didn't even know what they were.

I looked around the cavernous chamber. Rhys hadn't arrived yet.

"Rhys?" I said, looking up at her.

She pointed toward the door. I assumed that meant I was to go and fetch him. Tucking the binder beneath my arm, I hurried out of the chamber and along the tunnels.

I ran out toward the entrance of the cave and saw Rhys sitting on a boulder, staring out at the ocean.

"Rhys!" I shouted.

He jumped to his feet, a look of relief on his face, and climbed up toward me.

He held my hand and pulled me close to him.

"She wants to see you now," I said.

He gripped my hand and we walked back to the chamber.

The Ancient was still standing beside the pool, her thin arms crossed over her chest. She spoke up. Rhys looked at me. "She says you have a bundle of maps."

I withdrew them from my cloak and handed them to him.

He flipped through the pages.

"What are they?" I asked.

"Not now," he said, turning back to the Ancient. He

continued talking to her.

When there was a gap in their conversation I asked anxiously, "So what now? Did I pass her test?"

He looked down at me and nodded.

I didn't know whether to be relieved or terrified. At least now I would have Rhys by my side for the rest of the way. It just unnerved me that I still had no idea what this involved.

He pulled me down closer to the witch. Lilith was so freakishly tall she even towered over Rhys. I sat down on the floor beside the pool as they finished their conversation.

Finally the witch turned to me and, looking me directly in the eye, rasped, "Mo-na."

The sound of my name coming out of her decaying lips sent chills running down my spine. I stood up again and walked closer to her, gripping Rhys' arm as I did.

Then she said something else to me.

I looked at Rhys, my eyebrows raised. Even he looked reluctant to translate for me, hardly making me feel better about the situation. "She is asking, 'Are you ready to become a Channeler?'"

I nodded, even as my stomach churned.

She hissed at me again.

"She wants you to say yes," Rhys said.

I looked her.

"Yes," I said clearly.

She chewed on her lower lip and then gripped my hand.

She forced me down on to the floor and hissed at me again.

"Sit cross-legged," Rhys said.

I did as I was told.

Rhys bent down next to me and sat opposite me on the floor. He placed a hand on my knee. It wasn't often that Rhys betrayed fear, but looking at me beneath the Ancient's grip, now he did.

The Ancient's hands closed around my skull, her sharp fingers digging into my scalp.

An excruciating pain erupted from where she was touching me and ran down my neck to the base of my spine. I cried out. Rhys' grip on my knee tightened.

She spoke again, and then let out a harsh cackle.

I looked at Rhys through squinted eyes, tears of pain dripping down my cheeks.

"She says now is the time that you need to trust me more than ever.'"

Chapter 26: Kiev

Now that I'd dealt with my siblings, it felt like a heavy weight had been lifted off my chest. I wasn't completely alone in this madness. Although they were hardly enthusiastic, I trusted that they wouldn't betray me.

As soon as they left, I hurried back into the bathroom. Anna's head rested against the wall, her eyes closed, mouth hanging open.

I feared for a moment that I'd already lost her. I gripped her jaw and made her face me.

She was breathing lightly. She had passed out.

"Hang on, Anna," I whispered.

I picked her up in my arms and hurried back into the bedroom to place her down on the mattress.

I grabbed a towel from the bathroom and wet it with cold water before proceeding to wipe her face with it. I rested it on her forehead, and sat by her bed, holding her hand. Willing her to come to consciousness.

I kept changing the towel when it became warm. Helina came in briefly to hand me her perfume, but didn't stay.

After about an hour Anna came to. I breathed out in relief.

Her eyelids flickered open and she started coughing.

"How are you feeling?"

She laid her head back down on the pillow and looked up at me weakly. I wasn't sure if she could understand me. Although her eyes were open, they looked unfocussed.

"I'm going to go down and find some more food," I said.

She muttered incoherently.

I pulled the blanket higher over her, then left the room, sure to double-lock it behind me.

Of course, the lock would be useless if a vampire really wanted to come in. But I hoped nobody had any reason to. It was just there as a mild deterrent. If somebody knocked, they couldn't come in without breaking the door of a Novalic down. And few people on this island would dare do that.

I hurried back down to the kitchen for the second time within the space of a few hours. Relieved to see that it was still empty, I raced around trying to figure out what the hell I should bring up for her this time that her stomach could handle.

Soup was one of the most easy things to digest. But perhaps the soup I'd given her had been too rich. Or perhaps it had contained too many spices for her fragile stomach. Whatever the case, I had to try again.

Baby food is what she needs.

Unsure of what I was even doing—for I had always been a useless cook even as a human—I found a sack of vegetables and hurled them onto the counter. I dipped my hands into the sack and pulled out a handful of what resembled potatoes and carrots. *These should do.* I washed them, then I boiled a large pot of water and dropped them in.

I waited impatiently by the boiling pot, sticking a knife into the vegetables every few minutes.

These things take so damn long to get soft.

Finally, I decided that they were soft enough to not cause Anna more stomach upset. I dropped them into a bowl and began to mash them up together with a spoon. Once they'd formed a thick paste, I found some milk in the cold cellar and warmed a few cupfuls. I poured the warm milk into the bowl of vegetable paste. I grabbed some salt from the counter and added a few pinches. Then I blended it all together furiously until it formed a smooth consistency.

I poured the liquid into a large bowl and placed it on another tray. I also added to it another jug of water.

No bread this time. Let's just try this.

I cleaned up after myself, then rushed out of the kitchen and began walking up the staircase.

I thought that I might have once again gotten lucky by not bumping into anyone on the way up, but just as I was about to turn the last corridor to my room, Efren appeared round the corner.

He stopped short, a look of surprise on his face as he saw me. Then his eyes narrowed on me. He looked at the towel-covered tray I was holding. I was relieved when he let me pass in silence.

By the time I reentered my bedroom, Anna was taking deep breaths. I walked over to her and placed the tray beside her on the bed.

I felt her forehead. It was still hot. But at least she seemed to be slightly more conscious than when I'd left her.

Seeing that she was clearly still in no state to feed herself, I lifted her up to sit against the cushions. Taking the bowl and spoon, I began to feed her. She coughed at first, but to my relief she started lapping up the food I was feeding her.

I watched her closely as she swallowed each spoonful. I wasn't sure if it was just my imagination, but by the time she'd finished the bowl, I could have sworn that her eyes appeared less distant. She appeared calmer, more aware.

"Are you feeling better?" I dared ask.

There was a pause.

Then she looked up at my face and breathed, "You're my angel."

She's still delirious.

Chapter 27: Mona

I stared at myself in the mirror.

Apart from my eyes having turned a few shades darker, and my skin looking a bit more sallow, there wasn't much difference. But internally, it felt like something had shifted.

Although I was aware of why I had set out on this path—to break free from my life with Rhys—I couldn't connect with that motivation any more now that the Ancient had bestowed on me such a gift and responsibility. I couldn't even conceive of betraying her and Rhys. And I had no desire to leave Rhys any more. Rather, it felt painful when I wasn't in his presence. I wanted him. I wondered if his being there for me while Lilith inducted me had strengthened our bond.

It had been a few days since we left the Ancient's cave,

and I was still getting used to my newfound powers. Rhys was helping tame me. He said we couldn't return to The Shade until I'd got a handle on them. I'd already almost burnt our bed to ashes and made a huge crack in the wall.

Only once he was confident enough that I wouldn't wreck the place did we return to The Shade.

I looked around as we walked through the courtyard up the steps into the castle. There was nobody around. It seemed to be late. I'd lost track of how long we'd been away by now, although it felt like an eternity.

We reached our room. My bones and muscles were aching from exercising my powers with Rhys earlier that morning. I wanted nothing more than to lie down and fall asleep.

As I moved toward the bed, Rhys said, "Wait. We need to attend the ritual first. It starts in an hour. We're just in time for it. If you want you can rest until then, but I'll have to wake you—"

There was a knock on the door. Rhys went to answer it. His aunt stood in the doorway. Her dark hair was tied up in a tight bun. She stepped inside and closed the door behind her.

"I sensed your return," she said, eyeing me as I sat down on the edge of the bed. "How did it go?"

"Mona's one of us now," Rhys said, placing a hand on my shoulder and squeezing it.

Although Isolde looked shocked that I'd returned in one

piece, she didn't voice her surprise.

"Hm. Good." Her mouth formed a hard line as she looked me over.

"How have things been since we left?" Rhys asked.

"We've kept up the rituals, if that's what you mean. But there's something that I must talk to you about."

"Oh?"

"I just heard from Annora. The immune is missing."

"The immune?"

Isolde nodded, her eyes darkening. "While you were gone, and since Efren was in no mood to help me, I decided to take the Novalics to collect some more humans from Annora. Well, a day after our visit she discovered the immune missing."

Rhys' lips parted in disbelief.

"Of course," she continued, "we don't know for sure that the Novalics are behind it. It could have been one of Annora's vampires. But even if they did, I think it's best not to ask them outright. I'd rather we find the proof on our own before confronting them. If they have done this then we have a very serious situation indeed."

Rhys rubbed a hand against his forehead and stared back at Isolde.

"You really think they'd betray us like this? After all they've seen of us?"

Isolde shrugged. "I'm just saying that this is an

unfortunate coincidence."

"Hm," he grunted. "Well, we ought to get to the bottom of this as soon as possible."

"Yes," Isolde said. "Because we can't afford for something to happen to that immune. It would be a huge setback. We have to hope wherever she is, she's still alive."

"Have you told anyone else about this?"

She shook her head.

"Not even Efren. I'd rather keep this between the three of us for now. In case they are innocent, I don't want to place unnecessary doubt in people's minds. Annora is conducting an investigation of her own. There is one vampire she already suspects could be behind this, but she'll get back to me about this."

"All right," Rhys said, his voice low. "I agree. It's best to keep this between the three of us until we know for sure."

"Well, I'll see you at the ritual," Isolde said. "The Novalics will all be there as usual, of course." She turned on her heels and left the room.

Whereas previously I'd been feeling tired, now, at the mention of the immune being missing, I was as far away from sleep as I could be. I knew the importance of the immune.

"We need to start investigating this right away," I said, walking over to Rhys. "There's no time to lose. We can't afford for anything to happen to that immune."

He looked at me and a small smile formed on his lips. He placed his hands on my waist and drew me in toward him, kissing me tenderly on either cheek.

"You really have changed," he said, his voice husky. "You're finally aligned with us. With me."

I stared at him.

"Of course I've changed. You think I could have survived what the witch put my mind through without changing?"

He continued staring into my eyes, as though he couldn't have adored me more than at that moment.

"No, of course not."

***

I stared around at all the familiar faces in the cave as everyone filed around the ceremonial stone at the center.

I scanned the benches for the Novalics. They had arrived later than usual and also sat in different seats, further to the left than I was used to. Normally they sat opposite us.

Erik and Helina Novalic sat together. Then, next to the girl, my eyes fell upon another dark-haired, green-eyed vampire I had never seen before. He was clearly related to them. Their brother, I assumed. He must have been a new recruit while I was gone. I looked away from him as soon as he looked up.

"That man next to Helina, he's also a Novalic?" I asked in a voice barely louder than a breath.

Rhys frowned at me.

"Yes, Mona. His name is Kiev. Don't you remember I already introduced him to you a while ago?"

"Oh." No matter how much I racked my memory I couldn't remember meeting him. So much had happened recently, I must have forgotten. Clearly, he couldn't have made much of an impression on me.

So that's three Novalics we need to watch.

I looked back at Kiev Novalic, whose eyes were now fixed on the slab in the center of the cave. Even though the vampire wasn't looking at me, there was something about his presence that made me uncomfortable. It was hard to put a finger on. I just felt... disturbed. Restless.

I was relieved by the time the ritual was over.

"I suggest we stay back and wait until the vampires have returned to their rooms," Rhys said.

I watched as the crowd made their way out. Kiev was the first to rush out.

Hmm. Interesting.

Isolde also stayed behind with us. We were now the only three people left back in the cave.

"I suggest we pick a vampire each," she said. "We'll wait until they've fallen asleep and then search each of their rooms tonight."

"I'll check Kiev's," I said. Though I wasn't quite sure why. Perhaps it was because his body language had already piqued my interest, and he was fresh in my mind as he'd hurried out first.

"All right," Isolde said. "I'll check on Helina. Rhys, you're responsible for Erik. We'll all meet back in my room after we're done."

"Do you know where Kiev's room is, Mona?" Rhys asked.

I shook my head.

"It's on the floor below Helina and Erik's quarters," he said. "It's the first door on your right as you climb up the stairs."

"All right."

We glanced at each other once more and then each of us vanished.

I appeared by the staircase and eyed the door that was supposed to be Kiev's. I placed my ear against it. I heard the sound of water running in the bathroom. I assumed he was getting ready for bed.

I waited another hour or so, walking up and down along that corridor and checking his door again at intervals. Finally, all had become silent and I heard deep breathing.

I appeared inside. All the lights were turned off. I made myself invisible as I crept along the hallway toward the vampire's bedroom. The door had been left partially open, just enough for me to slip through without having to touch it. Once inside, I looked around the bedroom.

The first thing I noticed was the smell of women's

perfume.

Strange.

Kiev lay in the center of the four-poster bed, a sheet half covering his bare chest. He was perhaps the most handsome vampire I'd ever laid eyes on.

Again, I experienced the same discomfort I'd felt back in the cave. My throat felt dry and my heartbeat quickened.

I tore my eyes away from him and, forcing my mind back to the matter at hand, I continued searching the room. I ducked my head under the bed. I checked the bathroom. I walked over to the balcony doors and peered behind through curtains. Nothing.

Then I turned and stared at the cupboard a few meters away from the bed. That was large enough to store a body for sure. I eased the doors open and looked inside. Nothing but the vampire's clothes.

I scanned the apartment once again but it was clear I wasn't going to find anything. Slowly, I walked back toward the front door and vanished myself. Once I was on the other side, away from the vampire's presence, I could breathe more freely. I decided to walk the rest of the way to Isolde's room rather than transport myself there with magic, to clear my mind and gather my thoughts together.

Both Isolde and Rhys were already there waiting for me when I arrived.

"What took you so long?" Rhys asked.

"The vampire took a while to fall asleep." I sighed. "And I didn't feel comfortable going in there until he had. I wanted to be able to move around without him in the way."

"So, any luck?" Isolde asked, looking at me impatiently.

"I found nothing. You?"

They both shook their heads.

"Then maybe it is one of Annora's people after all," Rhys muttered.

"We'll have to see what she says once she's conducted the investigation. But I didn't think the Novalics would betray us," Isolde said. "We still don't know their older brother that well, but I doubt he'd put his and his siblings' life at risk by doing something so foolish. Of course, it's possible the Novalics have already destroyed the immune and hidden the body…"

We all fell silent.

"Well, there's not much else we can do while we wait for Annora's report." Rhys stood up and held my hand, leading me toward the front door. "We'll see you tomorrow, Aunt."

We left the door and made our way back to our own apartment.

I removed my cloak, then walked over to the bed and sat down, removing my shoes. Rhys stood leaning against the doorway of the bathroom. His cloak and shoes still on, he stared at me with heat in his eyes.

I raised a brow at him.

He closed the distance between us and pushed me down against the bed. He caught my lips and unbuttoned my dress. Slipping his hands behind me, he ran them along my bare back.

I held his head and stared into his eyes.

"What?"

He pulled me up into standing position, letting my dress fall down my shoulders.

"You have no idea how enticing you are to me now." He groaned as he ran his lips along my throat. "I want to complete us. We've delayed this long enough…"

Reaching into his pocket, he got down on one knee.

"Marry me, Mona."

I took a step back, a gasp escaping my lips as I stared down at a sapphire ring.

He wanted me. I wanted him.

Why wouldn't I say yes?

Somehow, I hesitated. Although I knew Rhys was the one and only man I would end up with, the idea of marrying him alarmed me.

I guessed it was just the way he had sprung it on me so suddenly. I felt like I needed more time for the concept to sink in before accepting his proposal.

Perhaps sensing my surprise, he reached out and held my hand.

"You don't have to give me an answer now, my love. I'll

wait until you're ready. I'll wait a thousand years if that's what it takes."

I sat back down on the bed.

"I think I just need some rest," I murmured. "It's been a long day."

He nodded and placed the beautiful ring on my dressing table.

We undressed and I snuggled up next to Rhys beneath the covers. I placed my head against his chest, listening to his heartbeat, while he stroked my hair.

We didn't speak the rest of that night as we drifted off to sleep. He gave me space to get lost in my own thoughts. But I was sure he already knew my answer.

Although it had come as a shock, there was nobody else other than Rhys whom I belonged to. He owned my heart and mind. My body and soul.

Chapter 28: Kiev

I'd been anticipating that anytime now, Annora or one of her comrades would notice Anna missing from the cells and alert Isolde.

The Novalics would be the prime suspects.

So as a matter of urgency I had to find somewhere safer to hide Anna. My room was the perfect place, because people were unlikely to venture into it for no reason. But it was also the prime target. I stalked up and down the room trying to rack my brains for some kind of solution.

The apartment wasn't huge and there weren't many hiding places. The cupboard spanning the entire length of one wall would have been perfect—it was more than big enough to hold her. It could have even fit me if I curled up my feet. But it was far too obvious a hiding place... But as I was staring at the wardrobe, a solution came to me.

I hurried upstairs and brought Erik down. He always had been good with woodwork.

"I want to section off the back part of this cupboard. Remove the back board, and cut this cupboard's depth in half, say. That way, Anna can lie behind it. If you do it right, no witch will suspect anything is behind it on a cursory glance."

He leant inside and knocked against the wood.

"Hm." He looked at the wood. "Well, let me try to remove this..."

His voice trailed off as he began to run his claws around the edge of the board.

"It's not fastened very tightly," he muttered. "If you go down to the kitchen and bring me up some kind of long thin knife, and also some kind of utensil with a blunt end, I'll have a go at this."

I glanced over at Anna who was sleeping.

"I won't harm her," Erik said.

I rushed down to the kitchen and brought up as large of an array of utensils as I could find in my hurried search.

Erik began undoing the screws and then ran a knife around the edge of the wooden board. Slowly, inch by inch, he removed the entire board until it was loose enough to be pushed forward.

He stepped out and both of us pulled the entire wardrobe forward. I slipped round the back of it and pushed the board *forward until I was sure that I'd left enough room for Anna to lie comfortably.*

I also checked the front of the cupboard wouldn't look odd in case it was opened. No, there was enough space to fill up with clothes.

Once Erik was sure that I was happy with his handiwork, he left Anna and I alone.

Although part of me felt guilty making Anna lie back there, it was the best I could do for her right now.

***

I lay in bed the morning after the ritual, feeling relieved that we'd found a hiding place for Anna. Mona and Rhys had attended the ritual for the first time in... I'd lost track of how long.

I had no idea where they'd gone, but wherever it was, clearly it had done something to Mona. The way she'd looked at me from across the flames, it was as though I was a complete stranger.

I'd thought this was just her way of distancing herself from me. But her eyes also appeared darker, or perhaps that was just the firelight playing tricks on my eyes.

A part of me wished that Mona hadn't returned. Anna had taken my mind off of her recently. But now the discomfort I felt seeing her again returned full force. That ritual couldn't have ended soon enough. As soon as it had,

I'd shot right out of the cave.

I knew now that Anna had to spend as much time as possible behind that cupboard.

I still had no semblance of a long-term plan, and given that Anna was so close to childbirth, I was just taking things one day at a time.

I was fighting a losing battle. But it was a battle I was committed to fighting until the bitter end.

At least Anna had stopped vomiting and was able to stomach the simple meals I was concocting. Her fever was gone too, and she was much more lucid. Although there were still times when she appeared to drift off, she appeared to be recovering.

I'd done my best to make the cupboard soundproof by adding extra cushions and blankets. Though of course, there was only so much air we could block off or she'd suffocate.

As I lay in bed listening to her breathing, a thought that had been at the back of my mind ever since I'd first swept her out of that dungeon circled in my mind.

Why am I doing all this?

Why would I risk my life and the lives of my siblings for some woman I barely even know?

I shut my eyes and lay there for hours as I searched the deepest parts of me. I sat up only once I'd found my answer. Or at least what I believed to be the answer—for my own mind could be a confusing and treacherous place sometimes.

Memories of a pregnant Sofia flashed before my mind. The beautiful redhead kneeling before me, tears welling in her eyes as she begged me to allow her husband to be by her side during her pregnancy. Begging me to have mercy on her unborn children. The sadness in her eyes as I'd punished her for even mentioning Derek Novak's name in my presence. The screams of her newborn as I'd snatched him minutes after his birth.

Somewhere deep within my black soul, I knew I was grasping at what had eluded me for centuries: *Redemption.*

Chapter 29: Mona

I got up early the next morning before Rhys had woken up. Untangling myself from him, I pulled on my cloak and left the room. I wanted a few hours to myself before I returned and gave him my answer.

I wandered aimlessly down the corridors, recalling the look on Rhys' face as he asked me the question I was sure he'd wanted to ask for years now. He'd looked happier and more nervous than I'd ever seen him before. I imagined how he'd react once I finally said yes.

I stopped walking, realizing that I had arrived on Kiev Novalic's floor. I absentmindedly placed my ear against his door as I passed it.

Silence.

Backing up against the wall, I slid down it and sat on the floor, staring at the wall opposite me.

I might as well do something useful.

Although I'd searched Kiev's room and found nothing, something about him still left me suspicious.

"Mona?"

I found myself staring up at Efren.

"What are you doing up here so early?"

He eyed Kiev's front door, frowning. He was still wearing his night clothes.

I stood up quickly, straightening my dress, and, remembering that he wasn't to know anything about our suspicions yet, said, "It's nothing, Efren. I was just taking a walk and decided to rest my legs."

He looked at me disbelievingly.

"You know," Efren said, placing a hand on my back and leading me away down the steps, "I've noticed Kiev behaving rather strangely recently. I caught him bringing up a tray to his bedroom. A tray that smelled suspiciously like normal food. I think he may be swiping humans from the dungeon and having more than his fair share of blood."

He raised his eyebrows, then continued walking on his way, leaving me staring after him.

So there's definitely something going on with this vampire.

Normal food. There was only one place regular food was prepared and that was the main kitchen on the ground floor.

I decided to head down to the kitchen and wait. I wanted to see for myself what this vampire was getting up to.

I returned to Rhys' room first to find him still sleeping. I walked over to the desk and scribbled down a note.

"I've got cause for new suspicions about the Novalics. I'll be gone a few hours investigating. I'll return as soon as I can."

I placed the note on my pillow, knowing that it would be the first thing he looked at when he woke.

***

Covered by an invisibility spell, I'd been sitting in a corner of the kitchen for a couple of hours before the vampire walked in. He made his way over to the pantry and returned with a handful of vegetables. Clearly he'd timed his arrival just before the cooks came in to begin preparing lunch.

I watched as he worked with furious speed, chopping the vegetables into small pieces. He boiled them, mixed them with milk in a bowl, then poured out the finished liquid into a bowl. Placing it on top of a tray along with a large jug of water, he rushed out of the room.

I vanished myself from the spot and reappeared in his corridor in time to see him come running up. He opened his door and slammed it shut.

I placed my ear against his door once again.

Heavy furniture scraped against the floor. And then came the sound of a voice I'd been expecting to hear all along.

A soft female voice said, "Thank you."

I breathed in deeply, thinking carefully about what my next move should be.

She was still alive. That was a relief. Now I needed to get her out of there as soon as possible.

I decided to just do this myself. Still invisible, I appeared on the other side of his door. I crept along the hallway to see the cupboard pulled out from the wall, a pregnant woman sitting behind it as she sipped from a bowl.

My breathing became heavier as I prepared myself for what I was about to do.

I manifested myself.

The vampire shot to his feet, his eyes wide with shock. The human choked on her meal.

"Mona?"

"Novalic," I said coldly. "This game is over. I've come for the immune. And I suggest you don't fight. It will only make things worse for you and your siblings."

I moved toward the human, but Kiev ran in front of her. There was no way I could reach her without dealing with him.

He towered over me, glaring down at me. Again, I experienced that unnerved feeling that settled over me whenever I was around him.

"What happened to you?" he asked softly.

"What are you talking about?" I snapped. "Get out of the

way."

"You don't remember me at all, do you?" His eyes darkened.

"I barely know you. I believe I was introduced to you briefly once—"

He lunged forward and brought me crashing to the floor. His full weight was over me as he pinned me down by my wrists.

As I was about to wield my powers, I froze, staring up at him. His eyes had turned red.

I couldn't fathom why, but watching that green give way to such a frightening red filled me with an overwhelming sense of loss. The sight left me more breathless than his weight crushing against me ever could.

It was like a fire I didn't know still existed within me being extinguished. A candle being snuffed out.

"Your eyes," I choked.

He continued glaring down at me, one hand closing around my throat. His claws scratched against my skin. He could rip through my throat in a split second, but I didn't fight back.

And I didn't understand why.

It was as if his change of color had made me lose all will to fight.

I caught the reflection of my own dark eyes in his crimson irises. And I remembered a time when mine had appeared brighter too.

I realized then that the sense of loss I felt was for myself.

I've lost something.

Who was I before I surrendered to the Ancient?

Why did I ever allow myself to sink into such darkness?

I found myself questioning everything I'd done since my visit to the Ancient, and suddenly it felt like it wasn't me who'd done these things.

What am I doing with my life?

I've lost my way.

And I think I even expected that this would happen the moment I handed myself over to Rhys.

I reached my hands up and wrapped them around Kiev's, trying to loosen his hold on me. Again, although I could have used my powers, I didn't.

The vampire seemed surprised that I wasn't attempting to fight back, and loosened his hold around my neck, though he still sat with his legs either side of my waist.

His eyes didn't leave mine for a moment.

What was it that I made myself forget before?

I remembered the morning after I had taken the potion. I had woken up with tears staining my cheeks.

Could it have been this man?

I thought of Rhys, memories of his proposal the night before flooding back through my mind. The knots in my stomach became tighter. More painful.

Suddenly everything about the path I was on seemed wrong. Forced. I felt trapped by my own actions. Bound up in rope. Needing desperately to be cut free.

Just thinking about marrying Rhys now made me feel sick to my stomach.

That is not my life.

Rhys' wife is not what I am.

"I knew you before, didn't I?" I breathed, staring up at the vampire.

He frowned, then nodded slowly, his red eyes gleaming against the embers in the fireplace.

He stood up. I climbed back to my feet and gripped his shirt, staring up into his eyes desperately.

"What am I?"

His jaw clenched as he tensed beneath my touch.

He gripped my hands and loosened my hold on him, taking a step away from me.

"I don't know what you are. I don't think I've ever known." He swallowed hard.

"Please," I breathed. "Help me."

His breathing became heavier. His fists clenched.

"You're the most impossible woman I've ever met. Stubborn. Aggravating. Downright insane… Yet you've lodged yourself in my brain like no other. And I have no idea why."

"I loved you?"

He scowled. "You had a strange way of showing it if you did."

"I loved you," I repeated. And this time, it wasn't a question.

He stared at me.

I closed my eyes. How I was sure of such a statement when I had no memories of this man, I didn't know. But I'd never been more certain of anything in my life.

He stood there speechless. I walked toward him and reached up a hand to touch his face. I brushed my fingers against his stubble, my breath hitching as I relished the feel of him.

When I looked up again, I was staring into emerald green eyes. Several shades brighter than I'd ever seen them before.

At that moment, my heart sang. My chest felt lighter. Hope filled my dark soul. And then came the memories. Flooding back in waves. Filling my clouded mind with the ecstasy, the bright sunshine, that Kiev was to me.

"I remember you now," I whispered, placing a palm against his chest, over his heart. "You're my mirror."

Chapter 30: Kiev

"You're my mirror."

Her words rang in my ears.

Her cool palm resting against my heart, I reached up and touched her gently, brushing strands of her hair away from her face so that I could take in the full beauty that she was to me.

"I see myself in you," she murmured. "I see my darkness. My struggles. My base desires. And I... I think that's something that no amount of magic can cover up."

Something Matteo had once told me came to the forefront of my mind.

"Of creatures who inhabit the darkness, there are two types. Those who revel in it, and those who fight to escape it."

Although sometimes I still had trouble believing it, he had said that I belonged to the latter group, and that was why he had given me a second chance.

Perhaps what Mona is saying is true. Maybe we mirror each other. Maybe she's also struggling to escape it and that's why I feel this inexplicable pull toward her. Why, despite all her faults, I can't get enough of her.

Maybe my search for redemption is shared by her, and she makes me feel like I'm not alone in this dark tunnel with seemingly no end.

I breathed out as realization dawned on me.

As I stared down at Mona's pale face, all the confusion that had been pent up within me ever since I'd met her began to crumble away.

We've both spent our years trying to piece together the scraps of life we've been thrown.

And now we have each other, even as we go down together.

At that moment, I wanted nothing more than to hold her. Kiss her. Feel her. Lose myself in her.

My need for her consumed me as I pulled her flush against me and pressed my mouth against any part of her I could reach. Her chest, neck, cheeks, lips. I groaned as I breathed in her scent. She placed her hands either side of my face. Her tears wet my cheeks as she kissed me hungrily. She crushed herself against me, her arms tightening around my neck as though she was drowning. And I was her life raft, even if I sank with her.

When we finally detached ourselves from each other, the reality of our situation flooded back.

I still didn't know why exactly Mona had tried to erase her memories of me, but nothing had changed about our situation. She still belonged to Rhys...

She drew in a sharp breath, gripping my hands.

"I have the power to break free from Rhys now," she said.

"What?"

"I was granted the same powers as him, the powers of a Channeler. He no longer has the same strength over me he did before. I... I can break free from him." She spoke slowly, as though the concept of freedom was only just sinking in.

"Break free from him? And go where?"

"Anywhere. Far away from here. I can free you too. And your siblings, if they want to come." She paused, her eyes widening. "But we have to be quick."

Her words sent my head spinning.

I looked over at Anna, whose presence I'd forgotten until now. Shock and anxiety was written on her face as she watched Mona and I.

Maybe we'll be able to return Anna to her family after all.

"Rhys proposed to me last night," Mona croaked.

That returned my attention to her.

"What?"

She nodded.

187

"If we are to escape, it has to be as soon as possible. Tonight."

Tonight.

"How do you suggest we go about this?" I asked.

She chewed on her lower lip and began pacing the floor, rubbing her temples. When she turned to me again, it was with nervous anticipation.

"Go now and warn your siblings that we plan to leave two hours after midnight, tomorrow morning. Tell them to wait by the second largest ship in the port—*The Journeyman*, it's called. A large dark brown ship. It's moored right next to the *Black Bell*. I'm still not sure why you stole this immune, but since you seem to be bent on protecting her, bring her too. You'll come down at the same time as your siblings. I'll meet you there. And once we're all together, I'll break through all of our bonds at once."

She reached up to kiss me once more before taking a step back.

"I need to go now. I've already been away too long. I'll see you tomorrow morning. Please make sure that none of you are late."

I nodded, although I hated that she had to leave me again so soon after I'd rediscovered her.

She vanished.

I looked over at Anna. She breathed out, clutching her stomach.

"Thank God," she breathed.

I had no time to waste now.

"Anna, I need to go and find my siblings," I said.

I pushed the cupboard back against the wall, concealing her in the small space once again.

"I'll be back as soon as possible," I whispered.

I rushed toward the door and, careful to lock it, began racing down the hallway up the staircase to my siblings' quarters.

I barged through Helina's door and was relieved to find both her and Erik sitting in the living room sipping on glasses of blood, deep in conversation. They looked up at me in alarm as I stormed into the room.

"Kiev?"

I explained everything as quickly as I could. They sat dumbstruck.

"Mona… Do you even trust her?" Erik asked. "What if this is all just a test—a trap to see if we're loyal to them?"

"I trust Mona," I said quickly. "I don't have time to explain. You just need to trust *me* when I say that this isn't some sort of test. This is real. And quite possible the first and last opportunity to escape this place you'll have for the rest of your lives. I'm leaving with her tomorrow. It's up to you if you want to come with us."

There was a silence. They exchanged more worried glances.

"We'll be there, Kiev," Erik said. "I'm trusting you that this is worth the risk."

I heaved a sigh. I'd been expecting it to take longer to convince them.

"Good. Now I have to return to Anna. Remember, whatever you do, do not be late. I'll see you early tomorrow morning."

I dashed out of the apartment and hurried back down the steps toward my chambers.

As I stepped down the last step leading to my floor, I found myself face to face with the last person on this island I needed to see right now. The ginger warlock, Efren.

"In a hurry, vampire?" he asked.

I brushed past him, but he reached out and gripped my arm.

With his other hand, he held up a clump of long ginger hair. He dropped it down on the floor in front of me.

"I should have had the sense to test her hair right at the beginning for traces of potion."

I stood still, speechless. Although I didn't let my face display even the slightest hint of emotion.

"And guess what I discovered? She had recently taken—or been given—some kind of memory-altering potion. You wouldn't happen to know anything about that, would you?"

"I'm afraid not."

"Hmm... Somehow, I just don't believe you, Novalic.

Nobody else on this island would have done this to my sister. I know them all too well. Of course, I can't prove to Rhys that it was you who did this, but it doesn't matter. Because I know it was you."

I brushed past him, but as I turned my back on him, he reached out and grabbed my shoulder. As his fingers closed around it, an excruciating pain shot through my body. My legs gave way beneath me. I looked down in horror to see that he had paralyzed me. I couldn't move them an inch.

"Don't worry," he hissed, bending down so that his face was barely an inch away from mine. "I'm not going to be the one to punish you and make you suffer. I'm going to leave that to someone more capable…"

He reached down and, as he touched my head, we vanished from the spot.

Chapter 31: Mona

Rhys was gone by the time I entered our apartment and he didn't return until later that evening. I was about to step in the shower when he returned. I stepped out of the bathroom, a towel wrapped around me, as soon as the front door opened.

"Well?" he asked.

"Nothing still," I sighed, leaning against the doorway.

"What was it that caused you to have fresh suspicions of the Novalics?"

"Oh, I remembered noticing Helina sneak behind the cave after the ritual. I thought I'd just go and check those boulders and caves near the beach to see if she might have hidden the immune there. But there was nothing."

"Well, it's good that you were alert enough to check."

He pulled off his cloak and started removing his boots.

I walked over to the balcony, looking out, trying to calm my rapid breathing.

He walked up behind me, sliding his hands beneath my towel and placing both hands over my bare stomach. He pulled me back against him, kissing my neck.

He paused. "Why do you smell of Julisse's perfume?"

His words bewildered me. I knew now that Kiev was making Anna use perfume to mask the smell of her blood. *But why the hell would it be Julisse's perfume?*

"D-do I? I have no idea," was the only response I could think of.

"Hm."

"I've been thinking about last night," I said before he started thinking more about it.

He ran his fingers through my loose hair, pulling my head back and pressing his lips against my forehead. I felt his Adam's apple move against the back of my head as he spoke. "Tell me," he said softly.

"I want to complete us, Rhys," I whispered seductively. "I want to have your children."

His heart beat faster against me.

I turned around to face him. His lips were parted slightly as he stared down at me. And then, to my horror, a tear glistened in one of his eyes.

I hadn't seen Rhys cry since he was a child.

I'd lost count of how many years I'd spent craving to see any kind of sign of humanity in Rhys. Any glimmer of emotion.

But now, I wished to God that he wouldn't show it. I wanted to think of him as dead to feelings. Dead to love. I wanted his heart to be made of stone, because then it wouldn't be broken when I left him.

He scooped me up in his arms and twirled me round the room, burying his head against my neck.

His smile. It was boyish and uninhibited. It was the smile of my best friend, whom at one time I would have done anything for.

My throat tightened as he bent down and tenderly kissed my lips.

He reached for the heavy ring on the dressing table and slid it onto my finger. It weighed down my shaking hand, but it weighed down my aching heart more.

Throughout all of it, he thought I was crying tears of happiness. When really, I was shedding tears of guilt as I imagined him waking up alone in bed the morning after the love of his life had finally agreed to marry him, with no idea where she'd gone. I imagined him passing the rest of his years alone in his darkness, never understanding why she'd deserted him on what should have been the happiest night of her life.

But I didn't belong with Rhys.

No matter how much he loved me, I never could return his love. He'd fallen too far and I didn't know how to save him.

He thought I was crying tears of joy as he wiped my face with his thumbs, showering me with kisses.

When really, I was crying tears of goodbye.

***

Rhys even excused us from the ritual that evening. He didn't want to interrupt our time together.

It was just as well. As it was, I was afraid that he might not be asleep in time for me to sneak out at two am. I came to regret telling him I'd marry him. I should have expected that he wouldn't be able to keep his hands off me.

But at about half past one, to my surprise, there was a knock on the door.

Rhys pulled on his robe and opened the front door.

Efren's voice came from the corridor.

"Rhys, I'm sorry to bother you at this late hour. But there's something I need to show you urgently in the spell room."

Rhys returned to the bedroom, looking at me apologetically.

"I'll be back as soon as I can."

He kissed my forehead and disappeared from the room.

I didn't think I'd ever feel as grateful to Efren as I did then. His timing couldn't have been more perfect.

This is it.

This is my chance to leave now. Forever.

I reached for a piece of parchment by the desk and scribbled down a short note.

"Gone for a walk. Needed some fresh air."

I left the note on my pillow. I was about to vanish, but then something occurred to me. I opened the drawer of my dressing table and rummaged around until I found the old leather binder I'd retrieved from the Ageless' palace back in The Sanctuary. I still didn't know exactly what these maps were, but they seemed important. Pulling on my cloak and tucking the binder safely beneath it, I vanished.

I reappeared outside *The Journeyman.* Two dark figures waited by the ship. Helina and Erik.

I looked around, frowning.

"Kiev and Anna?"

Helina and Erik exchanged worried glances.

"We thought they were coming with you."

Chapter 32: Kiev

Every limb in my body was now paralyzed. I couldn't fight against the chains Efren had bound me in. I just sat in that underground room, slouched against the wall, barely even able to support the weight of my own head.

Efren approached holding a white-hot poker. I groaned as he ran it along my chest, burning a cross into my skin. It wasn't healing, so I assumed that he'd put some other spell on me to hinder my body's natural healing capabilities.

As I was close to unconsciousness, he stopped his torture and left the room. Darkness clouding my vision, I stared at the two humans opposite me. One a young girl, the other an older man. Now my mind came alive with panic about Anna. She would still be trapped in my room. Assuming

Efren hadn't already sniffed her out.

I shouted out in anguish.

Mona and my siblings would be waiting for me and Anna by now at the port.

Efren appeared in the room again, and this time, Rhys was with him.

Rhys stared down at me, his eyes wide with shock.

"Novalic?"

"I found him in here, Rhys. I caught him snooping around. I'm not sure what he was here for exactly. Anyway, when he saw he'd been caught down here he made a run for it, but I managed to stop him before he made it out the exit. Now, I trust you'll do what's needed."

Rhys reached down and gripped my neck. He squeezed hard, choking me.

He stamped down on my limp knee, crushing it with his heavy boot into the ground.

"I'll take it from here," Rhys said.

"Of course," Efren said, not even bothering to hide the way he was leering at me. He vanished.

"It's a shame," Rhys said softly. "I never did come to know you that much, but I thought you would be like your siblings. Clearly I was wrong. You have let them down."

Letting go of me, he walked over to a cauldron in the corner of the room. He started pulling bottles off the shelves and tipping ingredients into the cauldron. He lit a fire with a spark from his palms.

"Out of respect for the loyalty of your siblings if nothing else, I'll make this quick."

Make what quick?

I watched as he stirred the ingredients.

"You must understand that we need to maintain the integrity of this place. It's sacred space. Therefore, I must present you as a sacrifice to our Ancients."

He crouched down next to the cauldron and, drawing a syringe from his pocket, drew some of the potion into it. Then he crossed the room and dug the needle into my neck.

As the potion entered my bloodstream, it felt like my skin was on fire. It itched unbearably, as though there were a thousand centipedes crawling beneath my skin.

"This will help to cleanse your system. And make you more flammable once we've removed your heart," he said casually, walking back over to the counter and putting away some of the ingredients.

Once he was done, he picked up a wooden stake resting against the wall in the corner of the room.

Raising it over his shoulder, he walked over at me and aimed it directly at my heart.

"Again, Novalic, this is all for a greater cause."

He brought the stake slamming down toward my chest.

I closed my eyes, expecting to feel it piercing through my flesh. Instead after a few seconds I realized that its tip hadn't even grazed my skin.

I looked up, perplexed. Rhys appeared to be just as shocked as me to see the stake frozen in mid-air, a few centimeters away from me.

"Step away, Rhys."

Rhys stumbled back.

Mona stood across the room, her eyes burning with anger.

Chapter 33: Mona

I'd waited for half an hour down by the port. When Kiev still didn't show up, panic had gripped me.

I'd rushed up to his room and found Anna still trapped behind the cupboard in a distressed condition. I'd transported her back down to the boat, entrusting Helina and Erik to look after her.

And then, remembering Efren coming and knocking on the door, a frightening suspicion had arisen within me. I'd headed straight to the underground spell room.

Nothing could have prepared me for what I'd seen when I'd entered.

After I'd halted the stake, all the blood drained from Rhys' face as he stared at me in shock. Although it hurt me just as much as him, I couldn't remain a coward any longer.

Holding out my palms, I sent him flying back. He crashed against the wall, his head smashing against glass bottles as several shelves came unhinged.

He didn't even try to get to his feet. He just sat on the floor, his back against the wall as he stared up at me. His breathing was shallow, his lips parted in disbelief.

I'd hoped that the day would never come when I'd have to go against Rhys face to face. I'd hoped I could just sneak away into the night and never have to witness the expression on his face that I saw now.

My powers weren't needed to win this battle. I'd already sliced through his heart with my lies and betrayal.

Even as I approached Kiev and restored mobility to his body, Rhys didn't budge. Although blood trickled down from his head, where glass had cut him, there wasn't even the slightest flicker of vengeance or anger behind his eyes.

Just hurt. Defeat. Confusion.

Emotions that had come years too late.

Emotions that killed me.

Tears spilled down my cheeks as I helped Kiev up the ladder toward the trapdoor.

"Goodbye, Rhys," I whispered, shutting my eyes tight as my voice cracked. The only comfort I could cling to was to hope that one day, somehow, he would break free from his self-inflicted chains.

But I'd hung around for too long to be willing to wait for him any longer. I just hoped that if he did break free, he'd find another person who could fulfill him the way Kiev fulfilled me.

Sobs wracking my body, I locked eyes with my best friend for the last time before we disappeared into the night.

Chapter 34: Kiev

We reappeared outside the port to find Anna and my two siblings waiting for us. My eyes fell on Anna. She looked in a terrible state as she moaned with pain. Although my legs were still unsteady, I scooped her up in my arms and we all boarded the ship.

"We need to hurry," Mona said, her voice still shaking. "Rhys might have let us go, but once Isolde and the other witches discover what happened, they won't let us go without a fight."

Erik and Helina set to work at the front of the ship organizing the sharks. We jolted forward so suddenly, I almost lost my balance with Anna in my arms. I headed toward the lower deck.

"Wait," Mona called. "I need to break your bond to this island before we exit the boundary."

Impatiently, I put Anna down and stood before Mona.

"Close your eyes," she said.

I had no idea what she was doing as she muttered something beneath her breath. She pressed her thumb against the center of my forehead.

"Okay, you're done."

I felt no different, but I trusted that she knew what she was doing. She hurried over to my siblings to do the same to them.

I picked up Anna again and took her beneath the deck. I ran along the narrow passageways. Looking in each of the cabins, I finally stopped outside one that contained a particularly large bed. I laid Anna on top of it.

"All right," I said. "Just wait—"

My sister's scream filled my ears.

Leaving Anna on the mattress, I raced back upstairs. My jaw dropped on seeing Rhys standing in the center of the deck, gripping Helina by the neck. Mona and Erik stood a few feet away, trying to reason with the warlock.

"No!" I roared.

I saw red and launched myself at Rhys. As he held up a palm, the breath was knocked out of me and I crashed back ten feet, landing on the wooden floor.

Incensed, I sprang back to my feet. "Why don't you fight

me like a man?"

Hatred burned in his eyes as they fixed on mine. Slowly, he loosened his grip on Helina's neck, and she sank to the floor, choking.

"Rhys!" Mona gripped hold of his arm and tugged him back.

"Get your hands off me, traitor," he spat, brushing her away. "Did you really think that I'd just sit back and let you all escape?"

He continued walking toward me and stopped a few feet away.

"Fight you like a man?" he said softly, removing his cloak and throwing it to the floor. "Nothing would give me greater pleasure."

Chapter 35: Mona

I stared in horror as Rhys approached Kiev.

"No!" I shouted.

Kiev was still injured. His legs were still unsteady.

"It's all right," Rhys said. "I promise to not use any magic with your lover."

He reached for his belt and pulled out his long silver dagger. At first I thought he was going to attack Kiev with it, but he dropped it to the ground. Instead, he stretched out his empty palm and manifested a small wooden stake.

"This wood against your claws," he said to Kiev. "I'd say this is man to man."

As I reached out my palms, about to curse Rhys, Kiev held up his hand and shouted, "No, Mona. Stop. I'll fight him."

"Kiev, no! You're not strong enough yet."

He ignored me and stared back at Rhys, the two men now only a few feet apart.

I watched with bated breath as the two men began to circle each other. Kiev extended his claws and bared his fangs.

Helina and Erik hurried next to me as we all watched with knotted stomachs.

Rhys made the first move in this deadly dance. He flew toward Kiev, gripping his midriff and sending them both crashing to the floor. Raising the stake in the air, he directed it at the vampire's chest.

Gripping Rhys' arms, Kiev dug his claws into his flesh until blood leaked through the warlock's shirt. Rhys grunted and sprang off him. The two men stood opposite each other again, breathing heavily as they calculated their next moves.

Kiev lashed out, attempting to knock the stake from Rhys' hands. But the warlock dodged him. Rhys caught hold of a rope that dangled from one of the masts and swung himself up onto the edge of the ship. From this vantage point, he stared down at Kiev. The vampire jumped up after him— both of them now balancing on the wooden railing. The two men didn't break eye contact for a second.

I gasped as Rhys launched all his weight at Kiev, causing them both to fall overboard. Erik, Helina and I ran to the edge. I scanned the waters. The two monsters resurfaced and began clashing in the waves.

"The sharks!" Helina gasped, pointing toward a dozen black fins protruding from the water.

Erik swore. We all raced to the front of the ship, attempting to rein them in. But the two men were so close to the ship, it was impossible. I climbed onto the wooden railing, staring at the sharks. I would have blasted them all out of the water, but the sharks were now circling so close to the two men, I might hit Kiev in the process.

And then it was too late. Kiev groaned. Blood stained the water. I screamed as Rhys gripped Kiev's neck and submerged him beneath the waves.

"No!" I shrieked and aimed a curse at Rhys. It missed him and bounced off the water. He glared up at me, and, to my shock, let go of the vampire. But even without Rhys holding him down, the vampire still didn't emerge. I couldn't even see the shadow of his form beneath the water any more.

"Kiev!"

Erik ripped off his shirt and dove in after his brother. I was about to dive in too, but Rhys climbed up the edge of the ship. He swung himself back on the deck several feet away from me. His dark hair dripping, he glared at me.

"You want to play with magic now?" he asked, his voice low, eyes glinting dangerously.

It was as if all traces of my best friend had vanished now and in his place was the ruthless monster I was used to.

Although I was dying to help Kiev, the time had come for me to face Rhys once and for all. I trembled as I threw my cloak to he ground. I could wield powers as strong as his now. My problem was I didn't have nearly as much control over them. I'd only had them for a short while and hadn't spent enough time honing them.

I held out my palms and aimed my first curse. He dodged it effortlessly. I threw another at him. Again he dodged it with ease. *Am I really so predictable?*

I recalled now how during trainings Rhys had anticipated my every move. *He knows me too well.*

He held up his own palms and a searing burst of light shot toward me. I put up a forcefield around myself just in time to avoid it.

"I taught you well," he muttered, leering at me.

I had to relinquish the forcefield as I sent another curse hurtling his way, but once again he ducked.

He raised his palms again and this time, a stream of thundering curses flew from them. I quickly put the shield up around me again, sweat dripping from my forehead from the force of his attack.

Don't break, Mona. You're stronger than this.

A scream pierced the air.

Helina lay on the deck about fifteen feet away from me, gripping her chest as her eyes rolled in their sockets.

No!

Panic gripped me. *One of Rhys' spells must have bounced off my shield and hit her.*

I vanished and reappeared next to where Helina lay. Although she needed urgent attention, I couldn't take my eyes off of Rhys as he began walking toward me.

Impatience was starting to show in his face now.

He's had enough play. Now, he just wants to finish the job.

Although Helina shook at my feet, I fixed all my mental power on Rhys once again. Pushing Helina out of the way, I raced toward the opposite end of the boat as far away from her as possible. Rhys followed slowly, clenching his hands as he walked. He leapt up onto the edge of the ship and stared down at me.

This is it now. I have to end him.

I recalled what Rhys had told me during training: in order to gain full control of my powers, I had to be free of emotion. Something that was impossible to do when I had no idea what state Kiev was in or whether Erik had even managed to rescue him.

As I stared into Rhys' pitch-black eyes, all the anger and resentment that I'd felt toward him over the years bubbled up inside me. Everything that I'd ever hated him for came to the surface. Taking advantage of my trust and friendship. Stealing away my innocence. Luring me away from my home. Cursing everyone I ever loved to die. Trapping me in a life that wasn't my own...

I expected the emotions coursing through me to have an adverse affect on my powers, as Rhys had always said they would. But a burst of renewed strength ignited within me. I was no longer struggling to maintain the forcefield around me.

His prowess seemed less insurmountable.

Whereas previously, I never thought I possessed the concentration to maintain the shield around me while also aiming curses, now I attempted it.

Even Rhys looked shocked as a fiery blast from my right palm singed his shoulder.

Closing my eyes and taking a deep breath, I willed all the strength I had within me to my fingertips. Once my hands were shaking for release, I let go.

It happened so fast, I could barely believe my eyes.

A raging ball of fire hit him square in the chest.

His eyes widened. His lips parted. His back curved and he lost his balance, falling into the sea.

I ran to the edge and looked down. His head bobbed above the waves, his body motionless.

He floated for several minutes, and when I still sensed no motion in his limbs, I rushed back toward the front of the ship. I wasn't sure if he was dead, but he was certainly unconscious. And that was good enough for now.

So long, Rhys.

I gasped on seeing Kiev sprawled out on the deck, deep

wounds covering his legs and arms. Erik was by his side, trying to feed him his blood.

"Erik," I said. "Get those sharks moving as fast as you can. We need to get away from here."

I turned back to face Kiev. The vampire looked up at me with hooded eyes. I fell to the floor and held his head between my hands, my tears falling onto his face as I kissed his salty skin. I ran my hands over his limbs, healing his wounds with my touch.

Although I wanted nothing more than to stay with him, now I had to help Helina.

"Your sister... I have to go."

"Huh?" Kiev climbed to his feet, following me as I hurried over to where I'd left his sister. When his eyes fell on Helina, still writhing on the floor, he opened his mouth in horror.

He crawled over her and gripped her shoulders. "What happened?" he asked.

Pushing Kiev aside, I sat down on the floor next to his sister and caught her head in my hands, studying her vacant—and now bloodshot—eyes.

"I'm not sure," I whispered.

Rhys had been firing so many curses at me, I didn't know which one could have hit her. Besides, curses often had a different effect on vampires than they did on witches. I worried that I might not be able to figure out an antidote in time.

But I had no time to doubt my abilities. I began muttering one chant after the other, trying everything I could think of that could mitigate the curse that was consuming Helina.

I must have sat there for almost an hour before, to my relief, her breathing slowed and her trembling lessened. Her eyes stopped rolling and after a few minutes she sat up, blinking and looking around.

"Wh-what happened?"

Curses could cause temporary memory loss, especially ones as powerful as Rhys had been throwing. Had I not become a Channeler, there was no way that ordinary magic could have saved her. I'd never thought I'd find myself feeling so grateful to Lilith.

"You'll remember in a few hours," I said, placing my palm against Helina's forehead to check her temperature. "For now, just sit down and don't do anything strenuous."

Kiev gripped her arms and helped pull her to her feet. He sat her down in a chair next to where Erik was navigating the ship. I looked down at the waves rushing past us. It seemed that the sharks had gained renewed strength from Kiev's blood.

I looked behind us, my eyes fixed on the spot where the invisible island was. Where we'd left Rhys floating in the waves.

Finally, I am free.

Chapter 36: Kiev

As soon as Mona had healed my sister, all I could think about was Anna. I rushed back down to the lower deck, dreading what sight might be awaiting me in her cabin.

"Kiev," she gasped, looking up at me as soon as I entered, her forehead covered with beads of sweat. "I think my water broke."

I swore as I realized she was right.

I ran into the cabin next door and ripped the sheets off the bed and also grabbed any other fabrics I could find—towels, curtains, anything absorbent.

Anna's eyes were shut tight as she contracted on the bed, her moans becoming louder and louder by the second. Covering her with a sheet, I assisted her in undressing. Then

I propped her up against her pillow.

I gripped her clammy hand, trying to calm her as best as I could. She squeezed me back, biting her lip as tears dripped down her cheeks.

"Please don't leave me," she breathed.

"Anna," I said, gripping her jaw and forcing her to face me. "I'm not going anywhere."

And I kept my promise.

I sat with her for hours as the contractions became longer, closer together and more intense. As her body started shaking and shivering. As she began to bear down. Even when Mona showed up to assist, I didn't leave. I was there to guide Anna when and how to push as the infant's head started to become visible. To hold her screaming baby boy in my hands. To hand Anna her child for the first time. To slit my palm with a blade and make her sip my blood to speed up the healing process.

I was there for her every step of the way.

The way I should have been there for Sofia.

Chapter 37: Kiev

Once I was sure that both Anna and her baby were in a stable condition, I caught Mona's hand and walked out of the cabin, leaving the two of them alone.

We walked up the steps and onto the deck above. We were now far away from the island. There was nothing but thousands of miles of ocean stretching out all around us.

I frowned on seeing the waves glistening in soft evening sunlight, even as our boat was shadowed in darkness.

I looked at Mona.

She smiled.

"Finally, I'm able to be of use."

Erik was still at the front of the ship, managing the sharks, while Helina sat in a chair next to him.

"Your brother had a few wounds too which I healed. But they weren't nearly as bad as yours," Mona said, eyeing my siblings. "As for Helina, she seems to be recovering faster than I expected."

I sighed with relief as I walked with Mona toward the opposite end of the ship. We both stood in silence, watching as the waves rushed past us.

And what now?

I pondered the question for several minutes. Perhaps Mona was doing the same.

"I need to find a way to return Anna to her family." I slipped my hands around Mona's waist, pulling her back against my chest. "But I'm torn, you see," I whispered into her ear. "Because I also finally have a powerful witch to deliver to Matteo."

She chuckled and twisted her head up to face me.

"Well, who says you can't do both?" she said, raising a brow.

I contemplated the two different tasks ahead of me.

I thought first of Matteo and Saira. I imagined what it would feel like to gain their trust back by having my siblings explain what really happened, and then presenting them with Mona. I imagined the smiles on their faces.

I just hoped that nothing bad had happened to them in the meantime. So much time had passed. And I knew how vulnerable they all were, all of them bundled into that ship without a witch. I badly needed to find Matteo and make sure he and his crew were safe. I needed to do this for him. But most of all, I needed to do this for Natalie.

On the other hand, there was returning Anna. She'd already been away from her family for too long, and she needed her husband. Even though it would mean a trip back to The Shade, I was determined to help her find a way.

Shivers ran down my spine just thinking about reuniting with Derek Novak, my sworn enemy. And now, my own blood. I wondered if the Novaks were still unaware about being related to the Novalics.

As I thought about the two undertakings, it was a matter of deciding which to do first.

Mona reached up and placed a soft kiss on my jaw.

"You don't have to make a decision right now," she whispered, turning around and placing her arms around my neck. "We can allow ourselves a few hours, I think…"

"You're right," I said, pressing my lips against her forehead.

She took a step back from me and hiked up her gown, revealing her long toned legs.

I frowned.

"Hm?"

She pointed to her right thigh.

I bent down to get a closer look at it.

Her black rose had disappeared.

She reached for my hand and pressed my palm against the spot where the mark had been.

"It means I'm yours now, Kiev."

Epilogue: Mona

Kiev and my story would never be a perfect "happy ever after", like the one I'd given my fictional characters.

We were both too broken. Our pasts were too tumultuous. Between us, we'd destroyed too many lives.

I knew we'd grate on each other's nerves. Our tempers would clash. We'd fight.

But this was one of the very reasons that we couldn't live without each other.

We could live without fear of bringing one another to ruin, because we were both already rubble.

Kiev was able to fulfill me in ways that I knew no other person ever could. And I dared believe that he felt the same about me.

He was my mirror, as I was his.

And I had faith that slowly, we'd help each other heal. It would be a painful ride, but I believed that we'd get there.

This story might not ever be like Adrian and Irina's.

But it was *our* story.

And, as Kiev claimed my lips while we sailed toward the deep orange sunset, that was all that mattered.

Dear Reader,

This is the end of Kiev's standalone trilogy.

I have thoroughly enjoyed exploring his character, and I hope you have too.

Kiev's story will now weave back into the *A Shade of Vampire* series, where his journey originally began.

You will meet him again in *A Shade of Vampire 9*. It's available on Amazon, or you can find details of this book on my website: www.bellaforrest.net

(However, if you haven't read any of my *A Shade of Vampire* series yet, I suggest you suggest you start with Book 1)

Love,
Bella

P.S. If you'd like to stay updated about my new releases, visit www.forrestbooks.com, enter your email address and you'll be the first to know when I have a new book out.

P.P.S. Also, don't forget to come say hello on Facebook! I'd love to meet you personally:

www.facebook.com/AShadeOfVampire

Printed in Great Britain
by Amazon.co.uk, Ltd.,
Marston Gate.